THEY CALL ME
Chief

Karl D. Keen

Author's Tranquility Press
ATLANTA, GEORGIA

Karl D. Keen/Author's Tranquility Press
3900 N Commerce Dr. Suite 300 #1255
Atlanta, GA 30344, USA
www.authorstranquilitypress.com

Ordering Information:
Quantity sales. Special discounts are available on quantity purchases by corporations, associations, and others. For details, contact the "Special Sales Department" at the address above.

They Call Me Chief / Karl D. Keen
Hardback: 978-1-965463-65-9
Paperback: 978-1-965463-35-2
eBook: 978-1-965463-36-9

Contents

Note

Though based on a true story the characters that appear in this book are totally fictional. Any resemblance to anyone living or dead is purely coincidental.

DIALOGUE

Johnny Two Bears was born on the reservation, he spent the first years of his life, living the customs of his people. After his father was killed his mother remarried and moved him to town, where he fought the prejudices and strange customs of the white people, torn between two worlds, that of the reservation Indian, and that of the white man. The love he has for his horse and living a part of his life with his grandparents on the reservation he seeks a vision quest to gain his own recognition, through many mishaps, and much turmoil, Johnny carves out his place in the two worlds he lives. His strong desire to become a leader gains him the nickname of Chief. A book for both children and Adults.

Dedicated

To

My Grandchildren

Stephen, Stephanie, Megan

Sarah, Audrey and Hope

May God always bless you.

CHAPTER I

I was awakened by the slamming of a door, in my sleepy haze I thought it came from the car. I heard a glass bottle rattle as if it had been kicked along the ground. I lay there in fear listening to the sounds. I could hear my mother saying something and then I heard my father trying to talk in a loud drunken voice. I knew then that soon this would be another drunken shouting match. I was scared of my father, especially when he was drinking. I was barely six years old and had been born here in this reservation house. A midwife had attended my mother aided by the neighbor lady Mrs. Crow. I guess Mom had a rough time bringing me into this world, but even at six years old it was nights like this, that I wished they had never made me.

I could hear their voices getting louder and things breaking. I wanted to get up and run into the sagebrush and hide, that was the only place I felt safe. There were places in the rock cliffs where I figured I could get away from the world and every bad thing in it.

My father used to be a good man when he worked at the mill. We had nice things and a good car, and he never drank. Then the environmentalist moved in and put a stop to the timber cutting. After that the mills all closed down and most of the reservation Indians went back to accepting the government handouts. There were no other jobs around and everyone became bored and began drinking to get through the day.

I lay there on my bed listening to my parents argue. The walls of these four room shacks that the government built weren't much. They had no electricity or indoor plumbing. Just a few gas operated appliances and most of the time the propane tanks were empty.

The sounds of their arguing got louder, I could hear someone kicking something, glass breaking and Mom's voice. I was afraid for her, she sounded scared. I thought I heard someone coming toward my door and slid off the bed on the backside and crawled under it.

I lay there in the dark afraid to breathe, I knew Mom would protect me the best she could, but Dad had hurt her several times when he was drunk. He would try and apologize for it when he sobered up. The door to my room swung open and I heard Mom say, "Leave the boy alone, he's asleep" Then someone hit the bed and I heard the old man say: "No one's here! Where's my boy?" Mom just stood there looking at my bed. She said he must be over at Billy's. Billy White Wolf was my friend; he was two years older then me and lived about a half mile from us. We spent a lot of time together playing in the rocks and sage brush.

Dad set down on my bed and I heard the sound of his shoes hit the floor. I could hear them arguing right above me. Dad was cursing really badly, like he was very angry. I was too scared to move. Mom went into the kitchen and I could hear her pumping water with the little hand pump that was mounted on the kitchen sink.

I could hear Dad's deep breathing. "Then he started snoring". I just curled up into a ball and tried to sleep there on the cold floor with all the dust bunnies. Mom never came back into my room she must have figured I really went over to Billy's, or else she was afraid to disturb Dad.

It was daylight when I awoke. I could still hear Dad snoring above me, quietly I slipped out from under the bed and grabbed my shoes and clothes, snuck out into the kitchen, got dressed and looked in their room, Mom was still asleep. The kitchen was a mess, I grabbed some bread put some jelly on it took an apple and crept out the back door. Billy would be in school today so I thought I would walk over to the reservation school and play with him when they had their morning break. It was about two miles to the school and I had to pass several houses on my way. The dogs all ran out and barked at me, but I knew most of them so I wasn't afraid. It must have been real early in the morning for I didn't see anyone. When I got to the school the door was closed and no one seemed to be there.

I walked up onto to a hill above the school to a place where Billy and I played. I liked this place as you could see for miles. It must be the highest place on the reservation; from here I could see several of the government shacks with all of the old rusty junked out cars parked everywhere. There were no paved roads just winding dirt and dusty tracks snaking out through the brush. Anyone who wanted to take a shortcut would just drive through the sagebrush over big rocks or around them until a road was made. "If you wanted to call them roads"

I looked back down toward the schoolhouse and saw that some of the kids were starting to show up; walking down the hill I came near the school and seen Billy as he came up the road carrying his books. He saw me, and before I could say hi. "He asked," "Where have you been'? Your Mom is looking everywhere for you." I told Billy about my Dad being drunk again. He all ready knew about it and said his old man had came home and passed out in the car. That he was still lying in the seat with his mouth open catching flies. We both laughed as I headed for home, knowing I was going to get a licking or at least a good scolding.

I met Mom halfway to the house; she just said good morning as she put her arm around me and gave me a little squeeze. I liked being close to Mom it was always a good feeling; she smelled like things from the kitchen and always had good words to say to me.

"Where did you go?" She asked.

"I walked Billy to school." I replied. She knew better but let it go. Finally she said: "Johnny" you know its not good for a six year old boy to be wandering around alone our here like you do."

I said, "Mom its ok, everyone knows me, and helps me if I need it." She asked if I spent the night with Billy. I told her no, that I hid under my bed when Dad came home. "I am afraid of him when he's drunk". Mom said, "Johnny! I would never let him hurt you, and I don't believe he would. He loves you very much. It's just that not being able to find a job really bothers your father. Most of the men on have no future that they can see. The mill gave them pride, as they all tried to out work each other, those were good times. Everyone played ball and had cookouts during the evenings and weekends. People were a lot closer then. Johnny I want you to promise me you won't wander off without telling me where you're going."

I hugged her and said, "Ok Mom." She squeezed me again and asked if I was hungry? I told her "Yes" even though I wasn't. We went into the house and Dad was sitting in the kitchen drinking coffee. "Morning son!" he said, as if nothing had ever happened. I guess to him it hadn't. I was beginning not to like my Dad. Why I didn't really know. He was the same man I had loved very much. I guess it was the drinking and the yelling at Mom I didn't like, and the fear that he put in me when he came home drunk.

"Want to go fishing" he asked? "Sure!" I said.

After breakfast we piled in the truck and drove over toward the lake that bordered the reservation. Dad had to stop on the way and get him a six-pack of beer, which ruined the whole trip. Why did he need to drink that smelly stuff? It always made him do stupid things. He would show off by picking me up, acting like he was going to throw me into the lake. Once he dropped me and I fell into the water. This scared him a little and he begged me not to tell Mom.

Dad was a big man and very strong. He had played football and wrestled when he was in high school, and was in the army serving in a place called Korea. He used to tell me how cold and miserable it was over there. He had gotten wounded and spent several months in a hospital in Japan. He was given a bunch of medals that he kept on the wall inside of a glass frame. I liked to look at all the pretty colored ribbons that they were fastened to. I once heard him tell Mom that he had lost all of his best friends over there.

The fish weren't biting very well but we did manage to catch a few small perch. On the way home Dad asked if I wanted to drive the pickup? I stood up in front of him and steered while he had a beer and helped me stay on the road. I don't think I made a very good driver. By the time we got home Dad had drank all his beer, and was going to go out and get more. Mom sent me over to Billy's so she could go with him.

Billy had just gotten home from school when I got there. He had to feed their horses, and chickens. We got the eggs and played with one of the dogs for a while. Billy's mom called us in and fed us hotdogs and kool-aid. After dinner we went up in the rocks behind the house and played until dark. We both went to sleep right away as it had been a full day. We were up early the next morning. Billy's mom slept in so we ate cold cereal and an orange.

We went back up on the rock bluff and watched a mother deer and her two fawns feed along below us. We decided to see how close we could get, moving only when the deer were feeding, we got down wind so they couldn't smell us. I was so close to one of the fawns I could almost touch it. I stayed crouched down in the deer brush while the fawn fed all around me. I could see the long eye lashes on it and the tiny hairs on its nose. I watched as it gently nibbled the tiny leaves from the plants. One of us must have moved or else the wind changed the old mommy deer snorted real loud and all of us jumped, then they were off bounding through the brush for a ways before they stopped. She snorted again and stamped her feet. We thought this was really funny and mocked her as we played along the rocks until Billy's mom called us for lunch.

After we had eaten the sandwiches and drank the milk she gave us I went home. No one was there. The house was cold and lonesome; I got an apple from the fridge. Everything in it was warm; I guess the gas had run out again. I sat there in a big chair by the front door and ate the apple. No one came home all afternoon. I was scared and lonely, and didn't like being home alone. It wasn't like being way out on the reservation; Out there in the brush I was never alone

There was always some animal or bugs to watch and keep me company.

I thought about going back to Billy's but I remembered that they were going into town for the night and stay with his aunt. As it got dark I shut the doors went in and lay down on my bed. I was too little to light the lamp so I just laid there in the dark and listened to the night sounds. Someone's dog was barking, and from a long ways off I could hear a horse whinny. The longer I lay there the more scared I became. Finally I got my blanket and slipped off onto the floor and joined the dust bunnies under my bed again. I felt safer under there. I was wishing I had a dog to protect me. Billy had a good dog. It was a mutt of sorts but it was friendly and liked to kill snakes.

I must have gone to sleep for sometime in the night I heard someone call my name. At first I was so sleepy I couldn't make out the sound, and then a flashlight shined on my bed. I couldn't see who was holding the light and I was too scared to answer, but as they turned to leave the room I recognized my grandfather.

I crawled from under the bed and hollered 'Grandpa!' I ran to him and hugged his leg. He reached down and put his hand on my head and asked, "Where were you boy?" I told him that I was scared so I hid under the bed. Reaching down and rubbing my head. He said, "You're a brave boy Johnny!" Let's get your a change of clothes. "You're coming home with me."

But Mom will be looking for me.

"She knows where you are, and she won't be home tonight." I liked staying with my grandparents. They had electric lights and a television. The picture was sort of snowy but you could make out enough to see what was going on. I liked the smell of grandpa's house. It smelled of sweet pipe tobacco and other good things that Grandma was cooking. She made fresh bread and always had honey or jelly to put on it.

Grandpa would take me on long walks out into the high desert. He would show me things that I had never noticed. He would hold open the pedals of a flower, and show me the pollen and all the stuff that the bee's gathered, show me what plants were good to eat and others that you could suck moisture from if you were real thirsty. Most of the juice from them was bitter but it would keep you alive. He made me a bow and we looked for feathers as we walked along. These he would glue to a straight shaft and make arrows for me, while sitting out in the sagebrush and chipping arrow point from a piece of obsidian. I wasn't permitted to do this as my hands weren't tough enough to keep the small sharp flakes from cutting me.

Grandfather always had time for me. When I would come into the room he would quit whatever he was doing and turn his attention toward me.

As we drove across the reservation toward their house he was very quiet. Usually he talked to me all the time. Finally he said, "John your folks have been in an accident. Your father wrecked his truck; he ran off the road over by the lake and went over a steep bank. He is hurt pretty bad. Your mom is banged up a little but she will be ok." I really didn't understand the seriousness of what Grandpa was trying to tell me. I asked; "Is Mom at your house?"

"No" "She is in the hospital, and we will go see her in a day or two. She will be all right." I didn't ask about my father. Why I don't know! I guess I was just more worried about Mom.

Grandma met us at the door and gave me a big hug, and kissed me on the forehead. "The boy was home alone hiding under the bed," Grandfather told her. Grandma put her hands to the side of her face and said, "Poor child!" Then she turned and walked into the kitchen. I stooped over and picked up grandfathers old gray cat that was rubbing against my leg. I liked to sit and hold him and listen as he purred when I petted him. Grandma told me to go wash and she would fix me something to eat. This made me very happy as I was starved.

I ate the roast beef and potatoes and drank a glass of milk. I was stuffed, but Grandma brought a hot apple pie from the oven which made me and Grandfather both happy. After supper she made me go take a bath and change my underwear. Then I sat on Grandfather's lap holding the old cat until all three of us fell asleep. Grandma made us get up and go to bed. I had forgotten my toothbrush. So she said, they would get me one in the morning and I could brush my teeth twice to make up for it. She laughed and tucked me into bed. The sheets on the bed smelled nice and clean. I liked clean sheets, we never had them at home, Mom didn't have a washing machine and it was too far to go to town to wash clothes. I mostly slept with one blanket or in an old sleeping bag if it was cold.

I slept well, and was awakened when Grandfather asked if I was going to sleep all day? Then I heard Grandma Say; "That poor child was exhausted and I don't know how long he has gone without eating!"

I got dressed and had breakfast alone. Grandfather was sitting out on the porch smoking his pipe. I liked the smell of the pipe; it smelled sweet like candied apples. I sat in the chair beside him. The old gray cat jumped up in my lap and started purring before I even petted him. We sat there in silence for a long time, just the two of us looking out across the reservation at the sagebrush and the small brown birds that were feeding on the grass seeds. A jackrabbit came hopping out of the brush. Grandfather said, "Better run old rabbit or you will be coyote feed." In a few minutes a coyote came around the same bush, seen us and ran back the way he had come. I asked Grandfather how he knew that the coyote was there.

He said, "I could tell by watching the rabbit". He wasn't looking where he was going; he kept looking behind him as he ran he jumped from side to side not straight ahead. By doing this, the coyote has to sniff out each side of the trail and the rabbit has time to get away. You can learn a lot about life just watching animals, and seeing what makes them do the things they do. People are a lot the same way, everything and everyone reacts to events in their life.

While we were sitting there, the tribal police drove up in their shiny silver pickup.

"Stay here." Grandfather said.

I sat there petting the old gray cat while Grandfather walked out and talked to the two policemen. I saw Grandfathers head bow as he turned and looked at me. I could tell by the way he and the two policemen looked that something was wrong. Grandmother came from the house and walked out to the truck. Grandfather put his arm around her and held her tight while he talked. She turned and looked at me with great sadness in her eyes, my heart filled with fear! Had something happened to my mother? I sat there and stared at all of the grown people. Grandmother started crying real hard, the policeman put his arm around her and they walked to the house. Grandfather had tears streaming down his cheeks, he looked old and hurt. Reaching out he took my hand and said, "Come in the house, Johnny."

Grandmother sat there in a chair crying into a towel that she had gotten from the kitchen. The two policemen stood and looked at me. Grandfather motioned for me to come over to him. I walked over as he looked at me with big watery eyes, and said, "Johnny your father died last night, I just stood there looking at him as tears ran down his cheeks, I had never seen him cry. The tears made his skin look so much darker as they ran in streams down his face. I guess I didn't fully understand all of this, I had seen dogs die and we had dug a hole and buried them. I had seen the dead deer, elk, and antelope that my father and grandfather had killed for meat. They always butchered them and put the meat in the freezer.

I stood there in front of Grandfather for a long time, finally I asked; "Will we have to bury him?" Grandfather pulled me real close to him and said, "Yes". "Yes we will." In my mind all I could picture was digging a hole and laying Dad in it. The thought of all that dirt being piled on him really puzzled me. The two policemen shook hands with Grandfather as he thanked them, and walked with them out to their truck.

"He was our only child," "I knew all the drinking was going to get him hurt. He just never was the same after they closed down the mill. I should have never raised him here on the reservation. Maybe if I had moved to town he would have gone to college and gotten a good job. I worked in the sawmill for forty-one years, and never thought it would close."

The policemen shook hands with Grandfather again, got in the shiny truck and drove away. Grandfather stood there looking out across the reservation. He bent over and picked up a handful of dirt and slowly let it slip through his hand. He watched as the dust blew away and the dirt fell back to the earth. He stood there very still just looking at the ground. Finally he looked at the sky and said something, then turned and came back into the house.

Grandmother had gone into the bedroom and was lying on the bed crying. Grandfather went in and sat on the bed beside her. I picked up the old cat and went back out on the porch, I knew that my father was gone now but I couldn't seem to cry. I felt lonely and sorry for my mother. Dad was a good man! He had just gotten trapped in a place he couldn't seem to get away from. He had been happy when the mill was running, closing that mill changed a lot of lives and I couldn't understand why they closed it. We still had a lot of trees growing on the reservation and the hills all over the country were covered with them.

I sat there on the porch holding the cat. I don't know how long I had been setting there when Grandfather came out and told me to go wash up, that we were going to go see my Mother.

We all three climbed into Grandfathers old pickup, Grandma was still crying and Grandfather's eyes were red. He seemed old and shaky as he drove into town where the hospital was. We parked in a lot across the street and walked into this large building. Grandfather spoke to someone at a counter and she pointed down the hall. We walked down and stood in front of these big doors. Suddenly they slid open and several people came walking out, we stepped into this small room and the door shut. Grandfather pushed a button on the wall and the room started moving, I grabbed hold of his leg and held on tight. He reached down and put his hand on my head and told me this was an elevator that took people up and down so that they didn't have to climb stairs. "I still didn't like it". There were no windows and it was too small, the moving room stopped and shook a couple of times then the door slid open again.

We got out and walked down this long hallway with lots of rooms on each side, all of them had people lying in beds. We stopped in front of a room with the door closed. Grandfather knocked on it then peeked in. He reached over and took my hand as we walked into the room. Mom was lying there in a bed with her head wrapped in bandages and her eyes were swollen and dark. She looked like she had been crying. There was a big white bandage on her arm, and a metal rod holding it up. She reached for me with her other arm. I was afraid to get too close until she patted the bed and told me to climb in beside her. Mom hugged me with her good arm, and gave me a kiss. She ran her hand through my hair and said something I didn't understand. The room smelled funny; there were bottles of stuff hanging on a metal post. I didn't like this place. Grandmother leaned over and kissed Mom and asked her how she was doing.

They sat and talked about Dad, and when they were going to have a funeral for him. He was going to be buried in the veteran's cemetery, at Eagle Point, Oregon. Grandfather asked Mom about Dad's discharge papers and stuff that he would need for the veterans administration. I gave Mom a big hug and told her good bye, she was crying as we left. Grandfather took us over to a big restaurant; I had milk and a sandwich while they drank coffee and talked. We drove over to another building in town and they left me in the truck while they went inside. I was asleep when they got back, I had locked the truck doors as I was afraid sitting out there with all the people walking by. Grandfathers tapping on the window awakened me; I sat up; sleepily looked around then opened the truck door. Grandfather asked Grandma where he should go next. She said, "We need to go by John and Mary's place" and get this boy some more clothes.

CHAPTER II

When we drove into our yard there was a light burning in the house. Someone had come in and cleaned. All my clothes had been washed the gas had been turned back on and the refrigerator was full of food, the beds were made and all the bedding had been washed. Grandmother said, "Well some one has sure been busy! We owe them a big thank you." Gathering up some of my clothes and put them in a box, Grandfather said he would buy me some new ones to wear to the funeral.

Billy's mother and Mrs. Crow came down and told my grandparents they had made the house clean for my Mom's return from the hospital, and that one of them would stay with her until she could manage things on her own. They both hugged Grandma and told her how sorry they were to hear about my dad.

Grandfather and I went outside, he lit his pipe as we walked around together out in the sagebrush, he told me that I would have to stay close to the house when my Mom got home in case she needed help with anything. He sat down on a big rock and stared out into the high desert as I stood there beside him he reached out and pulled me close and gave me a big hug. "You are the only son I have now Johnny. We will have to stay close and take care of each other. Soon you will go to school, I want you to study and learn all you can. This reservation is no place for a young man to live or raise a family. The only way out of here is through a good education. There are no jobs here except for the tribal police, and a few government jobs and you will need a good education to get them."

He knocked the ashes from his pipe onto the rock, and kicked them around with his foot to make sure they were out before we walked back to the house.

Mrs. Crow and Billy's mom were just leaving. Grandma handed my box of clothes to Grandfather then turned off the gaslight, as we got into the truck she asked Grandfather if he thought Mary would be able to attend the funeral.

Grandfather said, "I doubt it as she is pretty banged up and the funeral is for Saturday." We rode on to their house in total silence. The old gray cat was glad to see me I picked him up and sat in a chair on the porch. He began to purr as soon as I started petting him. Grandfather said, "Tomorrow we will go to town and see your mother again, and get you some new clothes. I have to go to the funeral home and to the Veterans office, you better go wash up and get some sleep, so we can leave early in the morning."

Grandfather got me up early and after breakfast we went to see Mom. The elevator ride wasn't as scary this time. Mom looked better today. She hadn't been crying but one of her eyes was still swollen and black and her arm had a big plaster cast on it. I crawled up on the bed and hugged her again. They talked about the funeral and stuff I wasn't really interested in. One of the nurses brought me a coloring book and some colors to use on it so I quit paying attention to the grownups.

We left the hospital and Grandfather took us to lunch. Afterwards we went to a big store and they bought me some new shoes, some shirts, and new pants. I had to try everything on. I didn't like all the dressing and undressing. We stopped at a grocery store on the way home, and they left me in the truck again. I sat there and watched all the new shiny cars and the people in them. Everyone seemed to be in a hurry like they were late for something. There was a big dog in the bed of a pickup next to us and I kept watching him, he kept looking at me and wagging his tail, I wanted to get out and pet him but I knew better so I just talked to him through the rolled up window until my grandparents got back.

They had several sacks of groceries that they carefully put in the back of the pickup. The drive home was quiet and I went to sleep laying my head over on grandmother's shoulder. She put her arm around me and held me tight. It felt good sleeping there in the comfort and warmth of the truck and with grandmother's arm around me.

When we got home I jumped out of the truck and helped carry the groceries into the house. The old gray cat was glad to see me, I picked him up and went back out to the porch and sat there holding him. He just sat in my lap and purred not going to sleep; suddenly he jumped up and took off around the house so I got up and followed him.

Grandfather was out in back of the house tending to his chickens. I helped him gather the eggs while keeping one eye on the old rooster. He liked to jump up and flog me if I wasn't looking, I asked Grandfather why he kept that old mean rooster he didn't lay any eggs and he was always jumping on one of the hens and mashing her into the ground. Grandfather just laughed and said, "He keeps the hawks away."

My father's funeral was the next day so we all went to bed early. Grandmother was up and breakfast was cooked and on the table when I got to the kitchen. After breakfast I had to go take a bath and put on my new clothes. My grandfather's brother and his wife came over in their big shiny car. My Aunt Sally and Grandmother got into the backseat with me, Grandfather got into the front with his brother. It was a long drive to the Eagle Point cemetery. I tried to sleep but there was so much talking going on in the car that all I could do was doze off once in awhile. When we got to the cemetery there were rows of white markers that Grandfather told me were put there to mark each grave. We drove around to the back of the cemetery and there were lots of cars and a tent set up with chairs and lots of flowers. There was a big shiny box sitting in front with a flag covering most of it with three men in uniforms standing to the side with rifles.

Suddenly this horn started blowing and the sound was so sad it made Grandma cry. I just held on tight to Grandfather and watched while wet tears flowed down his cheeks making dark lines on his skin. There were several people crying that I didn't know. A man in a suit got up and read from a book, he talked about my father and his time in the army and all the good things he had done.

Suddenly the three soldiers put the rifles to their shoulders and shot I almost jumped out of my skin! Grandfather reached out and held me tight as the soldiers shot the rifles several more times. Then the horn started playing that sad sound again. Off in the distance I could hear a tribal drum being played and someone chanting the death song. Two of the soldiers picked the flag up off the shiny box folded it one of them came over and laid it in grandmother's hands then stepped back and saluted.

Soon everyone got up and walked by the shiny box. They had lifted the lid and everyone was looking in. The man helped my grandmother up and held onto her arm as she stood there looking and crying. My grandfather picked me up and I could see my father lying there like he was asleep, he was wearing his army uniform with all the pretty ribbons and metals pinned on his coat. I could feel Grandfather shake as he reached out and touched Dad on the arm. I wanted to cry and to hug Dad but I didn't do anything. Grandfather put me down and we walked over to where uncle Del and Aunt Sally were standing with Grandmother. A lot of people came by and shook hands with everyone. Afterwards we walked back to the car and drove over to a restaurant in a town they called White City. I couldn't see anything white about it. Except most of the people we seen were white. So I just figured it was a white people's town, like the Indian reservation, where all the people were Indians. I was so hungry I didn't care what color the people were I just wanted to eat.

After dinner when we were walking out of the restaurant, I told

Grandfather that I didn't know that white people had their own towns. He asked me what I was talking about. I said! "White City" Isn't this place just for white people?" Everyone laughed at me! Grandfather said, "No this town was named after a man whose name was White."

I asked, "Was he white?"

Everyone laughed again. I still don't know, but they did make good hamburgers.

We drove back over the mountains to the reservation, and to Grandfather's house. The old gray cat was waiting for me. I sat on the porch and held him while everyone else went inside. Everyone decided to drive into town and see Mom. I went to sleep on the way to the hospital. When we got on the elevator there was a bunch of other people on it and I wondered how many people could ride it.

Mom looked a lot better, I jumped on the bed and hugged her and laid close to her while everyone talked about the funeral. I had a lot of questions but I would wait until Grandfather and I were alone to ask them. Mom said that she would be able to come home in a couple of days. This made me happy. School was out now and Billy and I could play all day.

I slept well that night as it had been a long day. I had a lot of questions on my mind but I forgot to ask most of them. Grandfather was out on the porch smoking his pipe when I got up. I walked out picked up the old and cat sat down. I asked Grandfather why the men at the cemetery shot those guns. He said it was a 21-gun salute to my father. I wanted to ask him about my father lying in that box but I never got up nerve enough to do it, so I just sat there holding that old cat and listening to him purr.

Grandmother called me to come eat breakfast and before I was done Billy came over. We got my bow and some arrows and went up on the hill to shoot digger squirrels. We shot all the arrows and could only found part of them. We had hit so many rocks that most of the obsidian tips had broken. We didn't hurt any squirrels but we sure made a lot of them run.

We asked Grandfather for some ice cream money and rode our bicycles over to the agency store. It was about a two-mile ride. We raced all the dogs that would chase us and had fun. The man at the store gave us the ice cream and wouldn't take our money. He said he would treat us today to celebrate school being out. He was a friend of my fathers and I think that was why.

Billy's mother came over to get him, and Grandmother talked her into letting him spend the night. We stayed up and watched television with Grandfather until we both fell asleep on the couch. Grandmother came in and made us go to bed.

It was raining the next morning and we had to stay inside. We did go out on the porch and play with the old cat and a piece of string until the cat got tired and lost interest. We pestered Grandfather for a while until he told us some stories about when he was young.

They used to make the young men go through a vision quest to get their names. Grandfather was called Blue Elk. He told us of sitting on a blanket up in the mountains all alone for twenty four hours without any food or water. He had to sit still facing the East. He wasn't allowed to move or make any noise. He had to listen to all the sounds and then tell the elders what he heard, and what went on behind him even though he couldn't turn around and look. He told us how scared he was and that some of the things he heard were large animals sniffing the air and walking close to him. He said that it rained on him during the night and when morning came a huge bull elk walked out from the edge of the forest and stood there looking at him. The old bull was almost white his coat was so gray and the rain on it made him look blue. The old elk watched him for a long time, shook his head up and down like he approved of him being there. He turned and faded back into the timber-leaving Grandfather there all alone. When he told the elders of this they named him Blue Elk. Still most everyone just called him John Elk.

My father had been named after him and I was named after my father. Billy and I wanted to do a vision quest, but Grandfather told us we had to be at least twelve years old. That this was part of proving yourself to show that you were a man, and that you could overcome your fear instead of running away.

Billy's mom came to get him in the afternoon and took Grandma to town to get my mom from the hospital. Mom was still pretty bruised up but she walked all right. After Billy left my mom and grandparents sat in the kitchen and drank coffee. I sat out on the porch and held the old gray cat wondering what things would be like without my father. Mom wanted to go home but Grandmother talked her into staying the night. I didn't really want to go home; it was always so dark and lonely there. The gaslights just didn't light up the room like the electric ones did, and I didn't like the garlic smell that the gas put out. I would miss my Father but I wouldn't miss the drunken fights and all the yelling that went on and I wouldn't have to be afraid of him anymore.

Summer flew by with Billy and me playing in the hills and sagebrush. We would sit and pretend we were on a vision quest. Only thing was we couldn't sit still more than a few moments then we had to look behind us.

School started and I went to school for the first time. I was in the first grade and Billy was in the second. We sat pretty close to each other and got scolded for talking the very first day. Our teacher Miss Scott was a small white girl not very old and kind of pretty, I think she was a little afraid to teach the Indian kids, as I could see the fear in her eyes and she didn't like to look directly at you for very long. I liked her and she worked hard to help each of us learn. She taught us about our own people as well as the whites and must have studied Indian culture, for she had an answer for most of the questions we asked.

At recess and lunch break we would run races. I was pretty fast and could out run most of the bigger kids, but Billy could always beat me. We had spent all summer running through the rocks and brush trying to catch baby jackrabbits, but they were always quicker and could dart about faster than we could.

I really liked school and my mom would help me read and do my spelling words, so I was always ready and seldom missed school. The year went by too fast. School was soon out and I was another year older. Billy's dad moved them to town as he had gotten a job with the forest service. After that I didn't get to see much of Billy, and I really missed him.

I spent most of the summer alone out on the high desert watching the animals.

There was a den of coyotes on the backside of the rocky ledge; I spent many hours watching the pups come out of the den and play. Their mother was always busy catching rabbits and mice to feed them. Once in awhile she would bring in a prairie chicken or some bird. I spent a lot of time feeding the pup's bread scraps and I could get pretty close to them but could never catch one. The old mother coyote ran at me one day and I almost got bit so I stayed farther back after that.

School soon started and it was nice to be back. I really missed Billy; his mother had brought him out to stay a couple of days with me. Mom has a new boyfriend, he is a white man named Bob. He treats me good, but I just don't trust him. He tries hard to talk to me, and took me fishing a couple times. Mom went with us once and it was a lot of fun. We went to some lake where the trout were big and easy to catch. "Even Mom caught some fish".

The school days were going by quickly. I liked the second grade and Miss Scott was good to me she explained things so I could understand them. I think she was getting more comfortable teaching on the reservation. I don't know where she lives, it must be off the reservation or over in one of the agency houses. They are a lot nicer than the ones we live in. All of them have electricity and nice lawns that are kept watered; it seems like all those people do is cut grass.

Mom was getting much better but she still limps when she walks. They have taken the cast off her broken arm and she can use it pretty good. We see Bob most every day sometimes he stays all night and sleeps on the couch. Mom likes him so I guess he is all right. He sure doesn't know much about Indians or their ways, but I guess I don't know much about white people either. There are two white kids that go to school with me but they are both girls and their fathers work for the agency. They can't run very good and are always so fancy dressed that I never see them play any running games. They just hang around Miss Scott and talk a lot.

Bob bought me a little paint horse, and we built a fence out behind the house and put up a small building with a shed roof off of it so the horse could get in out of the rain and hot sun. I was scared of the horse at first but I soon learned to ride him. I didn't have a saddle so I just jumped on him and rode bare back. I feed and water him every day and like to brush him. He likes that and will just stand there and let me brush him all over. He would always be standing at the fence when I got home from school. Mom always made me do my schoolwork before I could go ride horse. I couldn't think of a name for him so I just started calling him 'Horse.'

Soon school was out so Horse and I had all day to roam the high desert. Now I could go to places I had never been before out there. One day I rode Horse clear over to the big river it was a nice place and lots of green grass for him to graze on. I watched an old raccoon coming down the riverbank and a big jackrabbit got in his way. I expected to see the rabbit run but he stood his ground. As the coon came close the rabbit jumped at him and pushed him with his front feet then turned and kicked that coon in the face with both back feet. I never knew a rabbit would fight like that, soon the coon swam out into the water and left.

I played along the river and waded out into the cold water. I jumped and played like I was a rabbit fighting. Horse would stop eating and watch me. I guess he thought I was silly but I was having fun so I didn't care. On the way home Horse was feeling good and wanted to run so I let him go. I was bouncing around pretty good but managed to hold on with my legs and by grabbing his long mane I stayed on. We got home in a hurry. I watered and fed Horse, then spent about an hour brushing his coat until it really shined. I told Mom about seeing the rabbit and coon fight. She scolded me about going to the river and wasn't interested in the animal fight I had seen. Summer went by to quick, as Horse and I roamed all over the reservation and out onto the high desert. I didn't get to see much of Billy that summer but I had Horse and spent every day just riding around.

Just before school started Mom told me that Bob had asked her to marry him. She asked me if it was all right. This took me by surprise I liked Bob but I didn't know if I wanted him for a father or not. We talked a lot about it and just before Christmas they were married. I had just turned nine years old a couple of months before that and was now in the third grade. Bob and Mom moved to town so I stayed with Grandfather until school was out. He had a big field that Horse could run in and a nice barn so that he could be shut up at night when it was cold.

I liked living with my grandparents. I now had Horse and the old gray cat to play with. Grandfather would take me for long walks out into the reservation where we would visit some of the burial grounds. Grandfather knew where each grave was. There were no markers just a stone or a bush, this was sacred ground and not many people came here anymore. Grandfather talked to me about the wars, and the many fights they had with other tribes. He explained how it was in the old days. Each time before we would leave he would pick up a handful of dirt and face the East, North, South, and West and pray to the four winds letting the dirt slowly fall through his fingers as he prayed. "These things you will learn." He told me. "They must never be forgotten."

CHAPTER III

Summer went by too fast and I had to move to town and start school with all the white kids. There were a few Indian kids like Billy that went to school there, but he was in a different grade and a different room, so I only got to see him at break time and at noon. He had made new friends and didn't seem to want to hang out with me much anymore. I was the only Indian in my grade. The other kids didn't seem to like me much. I wasn't very big like some of the kids were, so I tried to stay out of the way. They played a lot of ball games that I didn't know how to play.

They would choose up teams and just leave me standing there. I was never picked to play on a team so I just did my own thing. I watched them play with a funny looking ball they called a football. They would run with it, throw it, and sometimes kick it to each other.

I figured out that the game was to carry this ball across a line without someone pulling you down on the ground. One day the ball was kicked over to where I was, so I picked it up and tried to kick it back but I missed the ball. All the kids laughed and made remarks about the dumb Indian. This really made me angry! Especially one big fat kid named Larry. He seemed to be mad at everyone and they all were afraid of him. I could see the fear in their eyes, as he would walk close to them.

He always pushed me every time I got close, he would call me 'Indian Lips' which I didn't understand. My lips didn't look any different than his or any other kids; soon all the boys called me 'Indian Lips'. I didn't like this school or the teacher I had. He was a little white man who wore glasses and seemed to be afraid of the kids. He wouldn't explain things to us. I tried to get Mom to let me go back to the reservation school, and live with Grandfather. She told me that I would have to go to another school anyway after the sixth grade so I might as well stay here and tough it out. I felt sick to my stomach each day as I walked into the room and heard all the kids calling me 'Indian Lips' and laughing about it. Mr. Smith the teacher never seemed to hear any of this. I really hated it especially when the girls would laugh at fat Larry's remarks.

It was noon break and I had just finished eating the sandwich Mom had fixed for my lunch when Fat Larry came over and asked what I was eating! "What are you eating Indian Lips, "Dog meat?" I picked up my lunch sack and walked away; he tripped me from behind and pushed me, and as I fell I remembered the raccoon and rabbit fight I had seen at the river. I got up and Fat Larry came up close to me. I pushed him hard in the chest turned and kicked him in that old fat belly of his. He was crying and screaming like I had killed him before he hit the ground.

One of the other teachers had been watching us she came over and grabbed me just as I had jumped on Larry and started punching him. All the other kids were gathered around; as I looked at them I could see the fear they now had for me on their faces. Billy was there and he came over and slapped me on the back, and said, "I sure am glad you finally gave old fat Larry what he had coming."

Larry and I both had to go to the principles office and he talked to us. He wanted to know what this was all about. I just sat there and never said anything. Larry was still holding his belly and crying a little. He told more lies in there than I had ever heard in a lifetime. I never did say anything to the principle, and then he made us shake hands and told us that he would not tolerate fighting in his school. As we walked back to our room, Larry threatened to hurt me real bad, but I didn't say anything. Then just as we got to the room he pushed me from behind. I turned around and kicked him in that fat belly again. Before he could do anything I butted him right in the nose with my head just like the desert sheep do when they fight. Big Larry's butt hit the floor and his face was covered with blood. You could hear him screaming clear through the school.

All of the teachers rushed from their rooms out into the hallway. I just went on into my room and sat at my desk like nothing had happened. Larry was lying out in the hall screaming like he was dying, and everyone was running around looking out the door. Mr. Smith just stood there white as a ghost I thought he was going to faint.

The school nurse showed up and started wiping the blood off Larry's nose, and the more she wiped the louder he screamed. I was scared at first then it seemed funny. I started laughing and all the kids looked at me like I was crazy. The more I laughed the louder Larry hollered, finally all the kids would laugh each time he would let out a scream. Mr. Smith was really upset; he came back to my desk and asked me what happened to Larry?

I had learned fast from Larry about how to lie. I told him we were racing to the door and Larry tripped and fell into it, just as I pulled it open. Mr. Smith left and later he came back and told me the principal wanted to see me in his office.

Mr. Schuler; the principal asked me what happened. I told him how Larry and I were hurrying back to our room and just as I opened the door Larry ran into it. He sat there for a minute and said, "His nose is broken did you know that?" I just sat there and didn't say anything, but there was plenty going through my mind. I knew Mom would be mad at me and I didn't know what Bob would do or say. Mr. Schuler wrote a note and put it into an envelope and told me to give it to my father.

I said, "My father is dead!" He sat there a moment then said, "Then give it to your mother." I took the note and put it in my pocket. At the afternoon break all the kids wanted to talk to me about Larry, but I just ignored them. Billy and I walked over to the edge of the playground where I told him how I head butted old Larry right in the nose. I told him not to tell as I had told the principal and Mr. Smith that Larry ran into the door.

Billy asked, "What are you going to tell your Mom?" I told him I would tell her the truth how he shoved me and called me Indian Lips, and how he had tripped me and pushed me down and how he had ran into the door. Billy laughed hard, and told me I didn't have nerve enough to tell Mom that story. He was right I would never lie to my mother. I wish I hadn't lied to Mr. Smith or the principal. If they asked me again I would tell them the truth. Grandfather had always told me how a lie dies a thousand deaths, but the truth only has to die once. I never did figure all that out, but I think I know what he was trying to tell me. I was glad when school got out. I took the note home and gave it to Mom and waited for the storm to hit. She very calmly asked me what happened. I told her the whole story and expected to get a spanking. She stood up, hugged me then asked me if I was ok. Turned and went into the kitchen.

When Bob got home from work I had to tell the whole story to him. He was disappointed in me that I had gotten into a fight at school, but was glad I had defended myself. So I didn't know if I was in trouble or not. It was Friday so they took me over to Grandfathers. I ran out to where Horse was in the pasture and he came running up to me. I took him into the barn and gave him some grain, then brushed his coat real good.

I wanted to go riding but Grandfather told me to wait until morning. I went up to their house and played on the porch with the old gray cat until suppertime. We ate and Grandfather and I watched some old western on television. It was one of those types of movies where the Indians always loose. I wonder if they ever have Indians writing any of that stuff. None of it was true. No Indian in his right mind would ride around and around a wagon train while everyone was shooting at him.

And I never ever heard an Indian yell and holler like they do in the movies. Maybe if they fell off their horse or something!

Anyway we went to sleep there on the couch with the movie playing. Grandmother came in and woke both Grandfather and me up and made us go to bed. Morning came quickly and I was eager to take Horse out for a ride.

I wolfed down my breakfast and caught horse. He was ready to go and wanted to run. I walked him slowly until we were away from the house then headed toward the river and let him go. He was running full gallop jumping tumbleweeds and sagebrush. It was a beautiful sunny day and we both felt good and the whole world seemed to stretch out before us. It wasn't long until we were several miles out into the reservation. Horse soon got winded from running so he walked and I let him pick his way. We rode up onto a rocky butte where I had never been before. There was a beautiful little valley up high and a little stream running through it with lots of wild flowers growing along the stream. I got off Horse and let him graze on the new grass. I sat and watched the honeybees move from flower to flower until they were all covered with pollen then they would fly straight up make a circle and fly off. I decided to find their hive. So I would watch one and see which direction he would go. I would walk that way for a while until I found some more flowers. I would watch until a bee left them and follow him some more. Horse quit grazing and soon followed me.

I saw where the bees were going into a small opening into the rocks. I crawled up there and moved some of the scattered rocks and found a small cave. I moved some more rocks and could see that inside it was a large opening. I crawled inside and could stand up in there. On a rock shelf I found the skeleton of someone. The skull was just lying there on the rocks grinning at me. I wanted to run at first but then I saw all the Indian mortar bowls, and knew I had discovered an old Indian burial site. I needed to leave as these places are sacred and shouldn't be disturbed.

About that time a bee discovered me and stung me on the ear. I headed for the opening with more bees after me. Horse jumped as I came running out past him waving my arms and swatting bees. Horse just stood there with his ears up looking at me like I had gone plumb crazy. About that time the bees discovered Horse standing there and went after him.

He jumped straight up into the air, squealed, kicked and came running past me jumping, bucking and squealing. He ran clear over toward the river before he stopped, looked at me and snorted real loud. I sat there in the brush and laughed at that stupid horse until my ribs hurt.

I walked down to where he was standing and caught him by the halter, snapped a short rope on it and led him out into the water where I could put some mud on his bee stings and mine. As we rode home Horse would jump every time a bee or fly flew past his ear. I almost fell off several times. I don't think ole Horse liked those bees. I put Horse in the pasture and brushed him off. I could only find a couple bumps on him so he must have ran real fast.

I told Grandfather about the cave and the skeleton in it. He told me to cover up the opening next time I rode over there, and only leave a small hole for the bees to go into. Also to use rocks large enough so that the coyotes couldn't get in there. I told him about Horse and me getting stung and how Horse had run jumping and squealing down through the brush. Grandfather laughed and asked me if I looked at the stings.

He said, "Sometimes bee stings can really swell a horse up." I told him I had put cold mud on the stings and they were just small bumps. Grandfather walked out to the barn with me and we gave Horse some oats. Grandfather looked at the bee stings and said he would be ok. Then he asked me about mine. My ear was a little puffy, and I had a knot on my head where one had gotten into my hair and stung me.

Grandmother fixed us dinner and I was really hungry. I ate until I was about to pop. We went out onto the porch and I petted the old cat while Grandfather smoked his pipe. We sat there until it was dark. Then Grandfather went into the house to watch the news on the television. Grandmother made me come in and take a bath, and go to bed.

I skipped church that morning, I told Grandfather I wanted to ride over and cover up that cave before something got into it. I had a hard time getting Horse to go near the cave. So I turned him loose, and he stood and watched me with his ears up and ready to run. I jumped and hollered at him and he turned and ran kicking and squealing like he was a rodeo bucking horse.

I carried a lot of big rocks up and closed off the cave so that you couldn't tell it was there, but I made sure there was a hole for the bees. I was careful not to move fast and get the bees excited. I really watched the bees coming out of the hole. The ones going in were too heavy with pollen to bother with me. I walked back over and called chicken horse and rode him over as close to the cave as he would go. He was too much of a chicken to get very close, so I called him "Chicken Horse" all day.

The day went fast. Horse and I traveled for miles across the reservation. I never seemed to get lost as there was a high flat mountain east of me and I could always keep it in view. I would let Horse pick the way most of the time. He would always get me home although sometimes I would think he was lost, and told him so many times. I don't think Horse listened to me much.

I hated to go back to grandfather's house, for I knew that my mom would be there to take me back to town. I had to brush Horse down and feed him before I left, and his stall needed to be cleaned.

Mom was there waiting for me so I worked hard to get everything finished. I didn't want to go back to town but I didn't complain as I knew it wouldn't do me any good. I said goodbye to Grandmother and

Grandfather, then went out and rubbed Horse on the nose and told him goodbye. I sat and rode very quietly all the way back to town. Mom tried to talk to me but I just didn't have much to say.

CHAPTER IV

It was now Monday and I hated the thought of going back to school. Mom had fixed my lunch, as I didn't like eating in the cafeteria, because all the kids sat and stared at me like I was some freak. I liked to eat my lunch outside and alone. Sometimes Billy would bring his lunch and eat with me. We would feed half of our sandwiches to the birds and squirrels that hung around the school playground.

Mom drove me to school, and I went inside and sat at my desk. Fat Larry came in and his nose was twice as wide as normal and both of his eyes were black. He looked worse than Mom did when she had been in the wreck with Dad. He stood there looking at me with a scared look in his eyes. I looked up and didn't say anything, but I had a big grin on my face. He turned around without saying anything and set down.

The bell rang and all the other kids came into the room. Some of them spoke to Larry and tried to make funny remarks about his black eyes. Then they would look at me like I was some mad dog or something.

After the incident with Larry the name calling sort of came to an end. A lot of the kids still called me Indian, or Indian John. Most of the boys avoided me unless I came close to them, then they tried to be nice to me. I think it was mostly out of fear. For they now know that neither Larry, nor any of them could bully me. I didn't look for trouble but I stood my ground. As far as being called Indian that was fine with me. I am proud of who I am, I know what I can do and don't need their approval to do it.

Mom always made me do my homework and helped me with it until I knew everything in my lessons. I made very good grades, which made some of the kids jealous. "I think" I tried to do my best and treat everyone like they treated me. Larry left me alone after that; he tried to stay away from me. One day the boys were playing football at lunchtime. The ball came over by Billy and me. We picked it up and ran at them throwing it back and forth. Soon all of them were chasing us and trying to tackle us. When they could catch one of us we would throw the ball to the other one. We could both out run all of them. All the days spent running and jumping the tumbleweeds out on the reservation made this fun and easy for us. We finally tired of this and gave them back the ball, but they asked us to play. It was the first time either of us had been asked to play football with them.

They made us be on separate teams, as I was about the only kid there that could catch and tackle Billy. He could catch me, but I could dodge him pretty good most of the time. It felt good to play with the other boys, and I looked forward to going to school after that. It is funny how one person like Larry can turn everyone against someone.

One day I told Larry I was sorry for butting him in the nose. "Is that what happened?" he said, "I always thought I ran into the door!" He laughed and I did too. We became good friends after that, and Larry quit bullying all the other kids too, so maybe it was good that I had done what I did to him. The days flew by and soon it was winter. I still rode Horse on the weekends, but it was too cold to go very far. Some weekends we would just go out to Grandfathers so I could brush Horse and clean his stall. I didn't like it when Grandfather had to clean it for me. He was getting old and I liked to do things for myself. Horse belonged to me and he was my responsibility.

I would soon be eleven and wanted to go deer hunting with Bob. We packed a tent and went up into the high Cascade Mountains. It was fun setting up the big white tent and sleeping on a cot, we had a stove in the tent so we kept good and warm. I stayed in camp and gathered firewood all afternoon while Bob and his friend scouted the hills looking for deer.

It got dark early so we sat by a campfire until I got cold, then I went into the tent and crawled into my sleeping bag, it was nice and warm in there. It seemed like I had just lain down when Bob shook me awake. He had a fire going and I lay there until the tent got warm. We ate a bowl of cold cereal and grabbed some apples and walked up the hill from camp. Jim, Bob's friend, went into the thickets below camp. We had just gotten to a place to sit when a doe and her yearling fawn came running past us.

We stayed there until the sun came up; suddenly Bob nudged me and pointed to a big deer coming up the hill toward us. I could see the sunlight gleaming off of his antlers; Bob asked me if I wanted to shoot it. I declined, as I hadn't shot the big rifle yet. We watched until the deer got close, then Bob put the rifle to his shoulder while I held my ears. I really jumped when the gun went off. The deer dropped right where he was. We stayed there and watched it for a few moments to make sure it was dead.

Bob showed me how to approach a downed animal, and how to make sure they are dead. He then let me help him field dress it. The buck had nine points on it, but Bob said it was just a four point. The two little points in the middle were just eye guards. You only counted the side with the most points, and you don't count the eye guards out west. He said: "Back east they count everything including the tail". He laughed and I did too, except I didn't exactly get what he meant. We drug the deer back to camp, and pulled it up on a pole, where Bob let me help skin it. Making sure I didn't cut myself. We put a white bag over the deer and hung it in the shade. Bob took the deer skin and scraped it clean then poured salt on it and rubbed it into the flesh side.

Jim came back in a couple of hours. I had gotten the campfire going again. Bob fixed us a sandwich and some cold pop. They decided to take a nap, and I walked down to the little creek. Bob told me to stay by the stream and not wander off. For a person can get lost easy in this forest. I made sure I marked my way even though I could still see the tent after I got to the creek. I played there for several hours making a little dam and I made boats from leaves off the old maple trees that had fallen. They were large leaves and I could fold them over and put a stick through them making a good boat.

As I walked back up to camp, I came upon a big range bull that was grazing between the tent and me. He stood looking at me, I was afraid and looked for a stump or log to climb up on, I stood there for a long time finally the old bull went back to grazing. I made a wide circle around him and was glad to get back to camp. I piled some more wood on the fire and sat there and watched it burn. Bob and Jim were both snoring in the tent and I laughed at the funny noises they made.

Grandfather had told me an old story about why people snore. He said: Back in the days when people lived in caves and had no doors they were in danger from animals attacking them while they slept. So nature made them snore so they would sound like there was a larger animal growling at them. That way they wouldn't come in where people were asleep, but go look for smaller prey somewhere else. It sounded like two great big animals growling in our tent. As soon as it got dark we left the guns in the tent and drove around with a spotlight looking for deer and porcupines. Bob wanted the guard hair off the porcupines for craft items that some of the Indian women were making.

We saw several large bucks that evening on a ridge across the stream from camp, so Jim decided he would hunt there the next day. I told them I would just sleep in and stay in camp the all day. I had been feeding breadcrumbs to the gray birds that Bob called camp robbers. They would fly down and take the bread right out of my hands. There were a lot of chipmunks around camp too and they were fun to watch. They would fill their cheek pouches clear full of pine nuts until they stuck out so far I thought they would burst.

Morning came and Bob lit the lantern in the tent I just covered up my head and went back to sleep. I could hear them talking as I lay there and dozed. Bob said "I think John has the right idea." and they both laughed. Bob told me to stay close to camp.

I said, "Ok" and went back to sleep.

It was getting late in the morning when I finally woke up enough to get up. The mountain jays were scolding the little gray camp robbers. I lay there listening to the sounds of the forest. I could recognize the sounds of some of the birds, but there were a lot of sounds I didn't know. I could hear the wind in the pine trees and squirrels chirping once in awhile I could hear a limb break or something fall from a tree. The jays were really getting noisy so I took some bread out and fed them. I stirred the campfire and put more wood on it. This caused a lot of smoke, and the wind blew it into the tent, so I just sat outside and enjoyed the sun. I heard several shots fired but couldn't tell for sure which way they had come from.

I hoped that Jim would get a deer as he had three kids and no job, so I was sure they could use the meat. I heard Bob's truck coming and walked out to where he parked to meet them. Jim had gotten a nice three-point buck. We didn't count the eye guards or the tail. Bob was giving him a hard time about how little it was, but after we skinned it I think it was as big as Bob's buck or maybe even bigger. I helped Bob scrape the skin clean and salt it down so we could make buckskin or rawhide out of it. Bob fixed us lunch; we had sandwiches, fried potatoes, and some canned beans. After lunch I washed up the pans while Bob and Jim went into the tent and lay down. It wasn't long until they were scaring off the wild animals again.

I walked down to the little stream to make some more boats, all the time keeping an eye out for that big range bull, I sure didn't want to run into him again. I saw several nice trout in the stream and wished I had brought a fishing pole. I knew Bob had one in the truck but I didn't want to wake him up so I just stayed and played with the leaf boats I had made. I watched a wild mink run along the edges of the creek poking his nose under every rock and into every little hole and crevice that he came to.

When I got back to camp Bob was awake so I told him about the trout I had seen in the creek. He got his fishing pole; we turned over rocks and logs looking for bugs, worms and grubs. We dug some fat white grubs out of a rotten log and went fishing. Bob caught a nice brook trout about ten inches long on the first try. We walked down stream to a beaver dam. Bob let me fish there and I managed to catch four trout out of there then Bob caught a couple more on the walk back upstream.

We cleaned the fish in the cold water then hung them on a stick and walked back up to camp. Bob fried the fish along with some more potatoes while Jim and I took the tent down and loaded everything on the truck. After we had eaten and everything was cleaned up we piled in the truck and headed back. I slept most of the way home, so it was a quick trip for me. We dropped the deer off at a meat-processing place, and took Jim home. Bob took the two skins and we put them in a tub of wood ashes and water, to make all of the hair come off. I had to go to school the next morning so Mom made me come in and go over my homework.

School wasn't so bad now that they didn't call me Indian Lips, and all the other names, but some of the kids still didn't want much to do with me, why I didn't know, but I didn't let it bother me. I tried to treat everyone nice. We played basketball in the gym now that it was so cold outside. I couldn't bounce the ball very good, and I never did make very many baskets, but I was quick enough to get the ball after someone shot it.

Billy and I got into an argument over how the game was supposed to be played. I was trying to tell him what the rules were, when he yelled at me and asked who made you chief? Everyone thought this was real funny, and they all called me Chief after that. It wasn't long until the whole school called me Chief even most of the teachers. I didn't like it at first until Grandfather told me it was a great honor to be called Chief by your friends. Only I wasn't sure some of those kids were my friends, especially some of the older ones, as I didn't even know what their names were.

Springtime came on quickly, and we could play outside and now we played lots of running games. These I liked for I could outrun most of the kids in school. I was getting to where I could stay up with Billy. We ran a lot of races and played soccer. I really liked soccer for I could kick the ball and control it good with my feet. A lot of the kids were afraid of the ball, I never worried about it hitting me in the face, it did several times and I got kicked several times by other players, I just took this as part of the game.

The weekend came and I got to go back out to my grandparent's house for the weekend. Horse was glad to see me, but his stall was a mess. I had to work until dark to get it cleaned out and then I took time to brush him good. I hadn't ridden him in a couple of weeks and he wanted out of the pasture, but I had to wait until morning. I grained him and put new bedding in his stall so he would still be clean come morning.

I slept well in grandfather's house, and got up real early Grandmother was up and fixed me breakfast. After I ate I put a bridle on Horse and rode him out onto the high desert. I loved the early mornings out on the reservation. The air was cold and crisp. Everything seemed so clean and fresh. All the plants were putting out their new growth, and there seemed to be wild animals everywhere. I would sit on Horse and watch the coyotes try and catch the yearling deer. Most of them got away but sometimes one would stand and watch a coyote while another one would sneak up on it from behind. I usually tried to stop this but I knew that they had to eat too. There were a lot of rabbits and mostly the coyotes ate them, as they were easier to catch.

The day was early so I rode Horse up into the high country. I had never been up in this part of the reservation before, there were lots of large trees and logged over areas that made a lot of browse for the deer and elk. I was getting near my twelfth birthday and I wanted to do a vision quest. I wanted to see if I could do it, so I picked a spot out on a rock overlooking the reservation. I tied Horse to a juniper bush which he didn't like, but I didn't want to walk home as neither of us had been up here before. Usually he wouldn't wander off too far unless something scared him. I picked a spot out on the flat rock over cropping and sat real still. I sat there for several hours not moving just listening to the sounds around me. Every time I would concentrate on a noise, my horse would blow through his lips, step on something or make a noise to break my concentration. I didn't know if I could sit for thirty-six hours alone out here or not, but I was going to try it as soon as the tribal elders and Grandfather would let me. I wanted an Indian name, being called Chief was ok, but I still wanted to earn my name, and my right of passage into manhood.

I untied Horse and to show his displeasure with being tied up, he bucked all the way down the hill, almost throwing me off a couple of times. I slapped him on the head and he took off on a dead run jumping tumbleweeds and sagebrush. I hung on tight and let him run until he was puffing wind big time, I tried to make him run some more but Horse did what he felt like, so he walked along like he was half dead until he was rested then he took off really fast, throwing me off behind him. He ran, jumped and bucked out through the brush then turned and came back to me. I wanted to get a stick and beat him with it but the way he looked at me I had to laugh, it was like he was asking me 'why didn't you hold on?' Sometimes I think Horse was smarter than I gave him credit for.

I was getting hungry so we headed for home. I ran Horse part way, and then we sort of trotted on home. I gave him some fresh water grained him and brushed him down. I let him out into the pasture and he lay down and rolled in the dirt like he thought I would brush it all off again.

When I came into the house Grandmother made me go take a bath and clean up before dinner. After my bath I went out on the porch and held the old gray cat while Grandfather sat and smoked his pipe. I asked him about the vision quest, but he just sat there smoking not saying a word.

Finally he asked; "Do you think you are ready?

I said, "I have been ready for a long time."

Grandfather sat there and looked out into the reservation, finally saying, "Son you know once you start on a vision quest you can't quit until it is over". If you do you never get another chance, and it is a great embarrassment to fail this. You must start preparing yourself both physically and mentally; this is not an easy thing. It takes a strong man to sit and not move for more than a day. Your thirst and hunger will make you suffer. You may hear things that you want to turn and look for. This you cannot do. Wild animals will come and walk close to you to see why you do not move. Birds of prey will swoop down at you. During all of this you must look straight ahead and record everything in your mind.

When your vision comes you must recognize it. It may only appear for a few seconds or it may last several hours. Think about these things I tell you son, for soon you will be a man, and a man has to make quick decisions, failing to do so might cost you or your family your life or your freedom.

I sat there petting that old cat and listening to him purr, finally I said, "Grandfather I will tell you when I am ready, and I will not fail for I will be prepared."

Grandmother called us in to eat. There was nothing else said about the task I had before me. After dinner I walked out and rubbed Horse's nose and thought about all Grandfather had told me. I would prepare for it and when my chance comes, I would not fail.

Sunday morning I slept late. Grandmother woke me and I went to church with them. I sat there in church, and never once looked around. I listened to the preacher, and tried to vision each thing he said so I could remember everything.

After church, Grandfather took us to a restaurant in town to eat. They sat and talked to some of their friends while I walked around outside. I wanted to go back with them but they took me home instead. Mom was glad to see everyone. She seemed very happy with Bob and he is good to her; so I am happy. At least I didn't have to hide under the bed anymore. I had to study my homework, and Bob helped me with some of the math. I am getting to like him better. I still miss my Dad he was a good man even if he did drink and do some crazy things.

He worked hard and provided well for mom and me. He served his country bravely and never asked anyone for anything.

CHAPTER V

Morning came and I was up early. I wanted to get to school and practice for my quest. I worked hard at sitting and looking straight ahead. I concentrated hard on each word the teacher had to say. I only looked around once during the whole first period and that was when someone's book fell off their desk behind me while I was daydreaming. At first break I talked to Billy about the quest, he said I was crazy to do that.

I told him maybe so, but you all ready have your tribal name and I am going to do it! I never mentioned it to him again. I continued concentrating more on everything I heard or seen. I found out that my schoolwork became easier and I didn't forget things like I did before. So even if I failed the quest I was gaining from getting ready for it.

Friday came and I went back to grandfather's house. I spent all evening cleaning Horse's stall and grooming him even though I knew I wasn't going to ride him the next day. I had other matters on my mind to attend too.

I went to bed and got up early. I left the house without eating, and walked about a mile out into the reservation. I found a small hill that was clear of brush and where I could see a long ways out into the high desert. There I sat down and stared straight ahead. I didn't have a watch so I never knew how long I was there. I sat and listened to the bees on the sage blossoms and to the screaming of a hawk as he flew overhead. Two coyotes came by, and one stopped and looked at me for a long time, then went on his way. I saw a small rattlesnake come crawling out from under the brush and coil up on a rock not more than twenty feet from me. I watched him lying there in the sun; I thought what if he crawls over here.

Do I sit still or try and get out of his way? This I must ask Grandfather. I could hear many sounds from what I believed to be insects or birds in the brush behind me. I never once turned or looked around. I got sleepy and dozed off while sitting there. I was getting cramped and tired of sitting in one position, but I didn't move. The snake finally crawled off the rock and went back into the shade of the bush. The sun was getting pretty hot now, and a fly was really bugging me, he crawled on my face and tickled my nose; I wiggled my mouth and nose as much as I could without moving. Beads of sweat ran down my face and I was getting thirsty. I must have been sitting there for several hours, as I could tell by the way the sun was moving that it must be past noon. I figured I would stay a couple more hours and then next Saturday I would do it again. I wanted to know that I could do it.

I sat there a little longer. Then I heard Grandfather calling me. I got up and walked toward him. He asked me what I was doing. I told him I was getting ready for my quest.

He said, "You are taking this pretty serious aren't you? John you don't have to do this now. Most boys wait until they are fourteen or fifteen. "Some never seek a vision."

I told him that I must seek a vision. I want to help lead our people; I don't want to be a follower. "I want to be a leader". After all they call me Chief.

We both laughed and Grandfather told me I could do anything I set my mind to.

He said, "I will talk to the elders and you can try for your vision as soon as school is out. I don't want anything interfering with your schoolwork."

We walked back to the house; Horse came up to meet us as we came by the pasture. I asked Grandfather if I could go for a ride, but he told me to wait until after dinner, so I went over to the porch and picked up the old gray cat. I sat there and petted it until Grandmother called me in to eat. After dinner I helped clear the table and offered to do the dishes, luckily Grandmother told me if I wanted to ride I better get going as it was going to be dark soon.

Horse wanted to run so I let him have his head; we flew out through the sagebrush and over the tumbleweeds, jumping several jackrabbits as we went. Horses ran hard for about a mile and as we came to the rocky ground he slowed to a walk and picked his way up a ravine onto a hilltop were we could see out across the reservation. Most of this was all open country just a few juniper trees, grass, and sage. There were no houses on this side of the butte. It was too windy and the snow drifted bad during the winter. Even the deer and the few antelope moved to the east side when winter winds came.

I rode Horse over to the cave where I had found the bees, nothing had tried to dig it out, and a few bees were still coming out of the hole. Horse didn't like it there, so I let 'ole chicken horse' run away. I didn't see how a tiny bee could hurt a horse much, but they sure hurt me, so I guess we both felt the same. I know I wasn't as chicken as Horse, at least I would go back and watch the bees. I only had a few more weeks of school left before summer break. I was now twelve years old and would be in the sixth grade next year. Billy would be going to junior high so I would probably be the only Indian in school again, anyway the only one in my grade, there were several Indian kids younger than me.

It was getting near dark so I took off for home as fast as Horse could run. Horse was jumping over brush and going full out, next thing I knew we were both going end over end. It really hurt when I hit the ground I lay there for a moment, then I could see Horse still lying down trying to get up. I forgot about my pain, and ran too him, he lay there breathing hard. I looked him over and finally got him to stand but he wouldn't put any weight on his right front leg, I felt it all over and didn't think it was broken. I walked and led him.

It was dark before we got home. I could hear Grandfather calling me before I got insight of the house; I answered him and told him Horse was hurt. He came over to us and looked at me and asked if I was all right. He looked at Horse and led him to the stall. sending me to the house. Grandmother jump up and asked, "John what happened?" I guess my face and head was bloody. She grabbed a pan of water and started washing my cuts and bruises. They hadn't hurt until now; Grandmother put some orange looking stuff on me that burned like crazy. She blew softly on each scratch after she put the stuff on. That helped a little.

I went back out to Horse's stall and Grandfather had put some liniment on Horse's leg and wrapped it.

He said, "If he isn't walking on it come morning we will have to call a veterinarian" I guess that is a horse doctor. He then asked if I was hurt. I told him I was only scratched a little. Then I had to explain what happened. I got scolded about running Horse when the light wasn't good. Grandfather told me that a horse has good sight and reflexes, but that the tumbleweeds could hide badger holes that could break a horse's leg, and that I shouldn't run him through the brush, but only out on open ground. He didn't think that Horse was hurt too bad, but that I shouldn't ride him for a few days just to make sure.

I went to church with my grandparents and I spent the whole sermon praying for Horse. I didn't even want to go out and eat, as well as I liked hamburgers. I went along but sat and prayed and worried about Horse until we got home. I changed clothes and ran out to the stall. I let Horse out, and he ran around the pasture jumping and bucking like nothing had ever happened. Grandfather came out and smiled, and said: "That is one tough pony" he is ok but you better not ride him until next week. I cleaned the stall and put down fresh bedding. I brushed Horse real good and gave him some grain, I unwrapped the leg put more liniment on it and rewrapped it.

Mom came over to get me, and of course I had to tell her all about the wreck Horse and I had. She just gave me a scolding look, and said "John you have to be more careful." School was getting to be fun now. We had track meets with other schools, I ran the hundred yard dash and won most every time, I also ran a race where you had to jump a hurdle ever so many steps. It took me a few times to get my steps right but after that it was my favorite event, and I never lost after that. I could even beat Billy. He didn't like to loose and would pout around like he was mad at me for a while every time I beat him. I was growing and my legs were getting longer. I was still just a skinny kid but I could run; and run I did, I ran everywhere I went. I wanted to be the best, I had seen so many Indians put down and talked bad about; I was going to show the world that I was as good as any man. And better than a lot of people that looked down on us.

I studied hard and put my grades before everything else, even the quest, and Horse. Grandfather had told me many times about the value of an education. How it was a way to get off the reservation and to help our people.

Sunday came and with it the spring rain, it was raining too hard to ride so I spent the morning cleaning Horse's stall. He didn't like being out in the rain and got in my way as I was cleaning. I kept pushing him out the door, and while I wasn't looking he bit me on the back. It really hurt, so I smacked him with the shovel, he got the message and ran clear to the end of the pasture and stood there with his ears and tail held high looking at me. 'Like why did he hit me? I didn't do anything,' sometimes I think Horse is crazy! He probably thinks the same about me. It rained all weekend, so I just sat and watched television with Grandfather and played with the old cat.

Bob came over and got me early as it was still raining. We stopped by the bowling alley, Mom was there bowling with some other ladies. I tried rolling the ball a few times but couldn't keep it out of the ditch; I guess they call it a gutter. I played some of the video games at the bowling alley and Bob bought me a hamburger, which was awfully good, and the fries were too.

When we got home, Mom and I went over my homework to make sure everything was done right. We were having a test everyday now, and I liked tests; they were easy if you studied and knew the answers. I liked trying to get better grades than the other kids. Some of the boys would call me a damn smart ass Indian, when I got an A on my test papers. I didn't mind, as it wasn't about being smart it was about studying and being prepared.

It was the last few days of school and we had a track meet with all the district schools. I ran the hundred-yard dash first, and Billy beat me by about a half step, I was slow getting started. My next race was the hurdles and I knew I could beat him in this race, so I was ready and when the gun fired. I dug out with all my power and almost fell, but I had regained my step by the first hurdle. I could see Billy right beside me in the outside lane. I completely forgot about him and just looked down the track at the next hurdle; I went over it in perfect stride. I tried to relax a little but keep my speed up, and as I came to the last hurdle I went over it with ease and with perfect balance. I then took a glance to my right, and Billy wasn't there. I crossed the tape pulling it out with my chest, it was then I could hear all the people yelling and cheering. I knew I had won but by how much. I looked around and some of the runners were just now crossing the line. Billy came up and put his arm around my shoulder, he said, "Injun you ran like some pale face was after you."

We both laughed, and then the teacher came up and told me I had set a new school record. I felt good about winning but didn't think much about the record, until I heard some one say something about me being in the fifth grade, and someone else said well he is twelve years old. I never thought about it for Billy was thirteen and I didn't care how old the rest of the kids were I still won.

On the last day of school we had a picnic, and played games. They gave out awards and I got several, one for the track meet and one for being a good citizen. What ever that was and I also got one for straight A's. There were a couple of girls got the same award but I was the only boy. I got called a smart ass Indian again, but everyone laughed when I was called it so I didn't feel bad. One of the girls was called Sandy; she had blue eyes and blond hair. I thought she was the prettiest girl in school. She came up and congratulated me, putting her hand on my shoulder. I was embarrassed at first, but it sure felt good so I stood there and tried to not let the embarrassment show through.

The other boys took off and started a ball game, I stayed and talked to Sandy, she lived in town not too far from us. I told her about Horse, and about riding him every weekend. She wanted to ride him, so I invited her over to Grandfathers to go riding. I could borrow a horse from my grandfathers' neighbor Mr. Black Fox. We always called him Foxy, but not to his face, he had several horses that very seldom got ridden. Sometimes Grandfather would borrow one and go riding with me.

Saturday morning Bob drove me over to Sandy's house and talked to her parents. He then drove us out to the reservation and to grandfather's house. We went out to see Horse before we went inside. I introduced Sandy to my grandparents and asked Grandfather about borrowing a horse from Foxy so we could go riding.

Sandy and I walked over to Mr. Fox's and asked about a horse, he led us out to the pasture, picked up a grain bucket, whistled and several horses came running. He asked me who was going to ride it. Sandy or me, I told him I would, so he caught a big buckskin gelding, he called Jake. He wanted to know if I wanted a saddle, I told him no, that we wouldn't be running the horses just riding slowly. We put a halter on

Jake and a saddle pad with a cinch strap, and I jumped up on him. Mr. Fox helped Sandy up behind me. She wrapped both arms around me like she was going to fall off. I sure liked that. To heck with Horse we would just ride around like this.

We rode back over to Grandfathers. Horse seen us coming and began running and bucking in the pasture, he came running up to the fence so fast I thought he would go through it. I Jumped off Jake, and helped Sandy down. I put a halter on Horse and a saddle pad. Sandy hadn't ridden very much so I was worried that Horse might act up with a stranger on his back.

I helped her on Horse, and held the bridle tight; he just stood there like he was asleep. Now I was really worried, what would he do next? Sandy asked me his name and I told her just 'Horse.' She laughed and said, "That's a silly name." I told her it was all I could think of that fit him. I led Horse out of the corral and he walked like he was on eggshells. I expected him to start bucking any minute. I was really nervous, and wishing I had just ridden double with her. If I had known how good it felt for her to have her arms around me like that I would have. I jumped up on Jake and started out. Horse just stood there. Sandy asked me how to make him go. I was afraid to tell her to kick him in the ribs so I rode over and took hold of the bridle and pulled him along a few steps. Ole dumb Horse figured it out, and walked along behind me after that. He still walked like he was balancing something on his back, and maybe he was! Anyway I was proud of him after that.

We rode for about an hour out onto the reservation, and then we rode down to the river and let the horse's splash and drink. I helped Sandy down, and she walked funnier than Horse did. I needed to use the bathroom, and I was in a real fix. I didn't know what to do so finally I told Sandy I had to go. That I would go over behind some bushes and look for snakes first and then she could go. It was embarrassing but I could see the relief on her face so I guess I did the right thing.

I hadn't been around many girls my age. Just the ones at school and I barely talked to them. I believe this was the first time I had ever been alone with a girl. Sandy told me thanks. She said, "I didn't know how to handle this"! We both laughed and talked about school and some of the kids, and things we wanted to do this summer. I told her I hoped she could come out and ride some more, she said she enjoyed it and would like to spend the whole summer out here.

I told her we had better be getting back. I caught the horses and tied them up while I helped Sandy up onto Horse. She was having a hard time getting on, so I just grabbed her and shoved her up onto his back. I didn't know where to grab and push so I just put my hand on her butt and pushed. She didn't say anything so I guess it was ok. I untied Jake jumped on his back and we started home. I tried to walk Jake beside Horse so we could talk, but the stupid horse wouldn't cooperate he kept slowing up or turning away. Finally I got close enough that I talked Sandy into getting off and getting on behind me. I told her I thought Horse was going lame. She stopped and slid off. I grabbed her by the arm and pulled her up behind me. She wrapped both arms around me, which was what I wanted. I turned Horse loose so he could follow us, now he wanted to run and play so I pulled the bridle off him, but left the saddle pad on. He took off jumping; bucking and squealing like a young colt.

Sandy said, "He doesn't look lame to me." I confessed and she squeezed me tighter. I was in love. I told her to hold on then kicked old Jake in the ribs; he really took off. I had to slow him down or loose Sandy; she couldn't hold on with her legs. Besides it would take longer to get home if we walked. It was a fun ride home. Horse finally settled down and walked along with us, giving me an evil look ever once in awhile. I do think he was jealous.

When we got home I stripped the saddle pads off and we brushed the horses down, then Sandy and I rode Jake double, back over to Mr.

Fox's that was good planning on my part as I got squeezed again. We thanked Mr. Fox and walked home. I held her hand until we got close to grandfathers house. I didn't want him teasing me so I pretended to throw rocks at things.

Grandmother fixed us a sandwich and we sat out on the porch and ate, the old gray cat came up and jumped in my lap. Sandy reached over and picked him up and petted him. We sat there talking until Bob showed up and took us back to town. We took Sandy home, and she thanked us and ran into the house. Bob looked at me and said, "Well?"

I said, "Well what?"

We both laughed and headed home. School was now out but I had some work to do before I could go back to Grandfathers.

CHAPTER VI

I was really tired and went to bed early. Bob got me up before he went to work and lined out all he wanted me to do. So I ate breakfast and mowed the yard, then got the paint and started painting the front fence. I hate painting and I get it on everything but what I paint. I took off my shirt as it was getting hot out, and you guessed it; Sandy and her friend Jill showed up. And there I stood the naked savage all skin and bones, naked from the waist up.

I excused myself and ran around the house and got my shirt, they were both laughing when I came back. Sandy teased me, saying Johnny you didn't have to get dressed on our account. I told them I had another brush if they didn't have anything better to do. They were going over to the park and asked me to come along. I wanted too, but I knew I had to get the fence painted. I told them I would come over later if I got all my work done. Sandy laughed and said, "Don't get any paint on your bare skin." I watched them walk away, and cursed the old fence that I had to paint.

I started thinking about my quest and lost all thought of the girls. I was worrying about how thirsty I would get or how hungry, and if I had to go pee. What if a wild animal came too close and I remembered the rattlesnake. I would ask Grandfather about these things before I started. It wasn't long before I had the fence painted. I was almost out of paint and Bob wanted me to paint the shed out back also. I started on the back of the shed and painted until I ran out of paint. I cleaned up the paintbrushes, walked out and looked at the fence, it look good even if I did paint it. I pulled some of the grass away from around the two trees in front, and the yard looked neat to me. I went into the house and cleaned up. I asked Mom if I could go over to the park.

The park was about five blocks away so I ran all the way over there. Sandy and Jill were still there; they were sitting on a park bench talking to two boys on bicycles. I didn't know the boys, but I walked over anyway. Just as I said "Hi" One of them said, "What do you want Tonto? The Lone Ranger ain't here." Everyone but Sandy laughed. She told him he shouldn't talk to me that way.

He said, "They should keep those blanket ass Indians on the reservation." I turned to walk away and the other boy said, "Hell he ain't red, he's yellow." I wasn't looking for trouble, and if Sandy hadn't been watching all this I would have left. I walked over to the two boys put my foot up, and kicked the closest one over on his bike he came up full of fight. I hit him my best-shot right in the face, I could see the fear written all over it, and I knew he wouldn't hurt me by himself. The other boy threw his bike down and jumped on me, throwing me to the ground. Sandy and Jill were shouting, "Stop it!" As I tried to get up both boys were punching on me. I was hitting and kicking for all I was worth, but I was still taking a beating. I was mad and scared; I could taste blood in my mouth, and the punches they were hitting me with, were hurting. I kept fighting back as hard as I could.

Suddenly one of the boys yelled, and now there was only one on me. I grabbed for him as he stood up, but missed. I jumped to my feet too, but both boys were lying on the ground holding their faces, and big Larry was standing there kicking one of them. He yelled, "You two yellow bastards want to jump on someone jump on me." Then he kicked them both again. They got up grabbed their bicycles and rode off; one of them said something to Larry; he picked up a stick and threw it at them, then turned to me and said, "Chief I can't leave you alone very long without you getting into trouble. What was that all about?"

I went into the men's restroom and looked at my face my lip was puffed out, about an inch, my nose was red and trickling blood, and I had one eye that was going to be pretty black, as it was really swelled out. I got a paper towel and soaked it in cold water and held it onto my eye. I was a mess, then I started shaking and wanted to cry, but Larry came in about that time and asked, "Chief are you ok?" My whole face was puffy; they must have hit me a lot more times than I remembered. I stayed in the restroom washing my face and holding a cold wet towel on my swollen eye, which was now turning purple.

When I came out Sandy and her friend were gone; there was just Larry and I, and so I had to explain to him what happened. He told me that those two always looked for trouble, and that I had better stay away from them if I was alone. I thanked him, and said, "I might have gotten my butt whipped, if you hadn't come along."

He put his hand on my shoulder and said, "Chief you GOT your butt whipped". We both laughed. I was afraid to go home, for I knew Mom was going to get all over me, and Bob would chew on me too. My heart was still pounding and I was shaking, I wish I had of just walked away, but Sandy would have thought I was a coward, if she had known how scared I had been, she still would. Now I was embarrassed, what would I tell Grandfather, and the tribal elders, when I went for my quest? I decided that I would just tell the truth and suffer the consequences.

By the time I got home my eye was really swelled up and purple. My whole face was real puffy. Mom noticed as soon as I walked in the door. She jumped up and said, "John what happened to you?" I almost lost it and just about cried. I told her how I got into a fight with two boys I didn't know, and how Larry had helped me. I told her the whole story. She got mad and called the city police, so one of the city police officers came out and talked to me. I told him what happened and that I probably started it by kicking the bicycle over with the kid on it; after the boy called me Tonto and a coward.

He said, "I think I know the two boys that were involved. If you press charges they will do the same on you. I will go have a talk with them, and if they ever bother you again come back and talk to me. And John I appreciate you telling me the truth, and for taking responsibility for your part in it". He got up and shook my hand. Mom walked out to the car with him and they talked for a long time. I was still shaking and felt all jittery inside.

The phone started ringing, so I answered it. It was the mother of one of the boys and she wanted to talk to Mom, but she asked me if I was all right. I said, "I think so, I feel kind of sick, and my eye is black." Mom came in and I gave her the phone and went outside and sat on the porch. I could hear Mom talking rather loudly on the phone at times, but I couldn't make out what she was saying.

I had been sitting on the porch for a long time when a car pulled up; a lady and one of the boys I had fought with got out, she was pushing him in front of her. I just sat there looking at them and didn't say a word. Mom came to the door and the lady made the boy sit there with me while she went in and talked to my mom. I looked over at him and he had a puffy lip, and his nose was twice as big as it used to be.

I sat there and looked at him. He wouldn't look at me. He just kept looking at the floor. Finally I said, "I'm sorry, I should never have kicked your bike over."

He looked up and said, "Does your eye hurt?

I said, "Yes! especially when I blink it".

He said, "I'm sorry too. We were just showing off for the girls". I told him I probably was too, and if they hadn't been there I wouldn't have paid any attention to what you guys said. I told him my name was Johnny, he laughed and said, "Really! My name is John." We shook hands, and it was then that I noticed how swelled and cut my knuckles were; I must have really been pounding on something or someone. John touched his swollen nose and said, "I think you broke it."

I said, "Big Larry probably did that."

"No he only threw me off you, and kicked me in the butt." We both laughed again.

Mom and the lady came out and stood and talked to us and made us shake hands again, and they both chewed on us some more. We stood there with our heads down and didn't say anything. John looked up at me and winked, and I laughed, which really made Mom mad. She said, "John this isn't funny."

I said, "It would be if it didn't hurt so much". We both laughed and finally both our mom's did too. They made us apologize, and told us this would not ever happen again. John said, "I hope it don't. My nose can't take anymore." and we all laughed. They said goodbye, and I felt a lot better after they had left.

I wanted to go over to Grandfathers, but Mom told me I could just stay home today and think about what I had done. She told me to go sit on the porch for a couple of hours and think about it.

I had been sitting on the porch for about an hour, when Sandy come riding up on her bicycle. She asked if I wanted to go for a ride, but I told her I couldn't; that I was grounded. She got off the bike and came and sat on the porch with me. She reached out and touched my eye and asked me if it hurt. I told her only when someone touches it.

She said, "John that was a dumb thing to do, especially when there were two of them."

I said, "Oh well! I was just trying to impress some girl. What was her name? Jill? Wasn't that it?"

She said, "Are you trying to get the other eye blacked?" and we both laughed. She said, "I was really scared."

I said, "Yea? me too. I was sure glad big Larry showed up when he did. I might have gotten hurt."

We talked about going out to Grandfathers and going riding again.

I told her that would be fun especially if Horse came up lame again.

She said, "I don't think he was lame before. You just wanted me to put my arms around you." I told her that might be true but it sure is safer to ride like that. You hold onto me, to keep from falling off; and you hold me on so I don't fall off. We both laughed, and I walked her out to her bike. She said, "I will call you tomorrow and maybe we can both go ride Horse."

Bob got home about this time. He took one look at me and asked. "What did the other guy look like?"

I said "Two other guys and they didn't look this bad." He sat his lunch pail down and sat down on the porch and asked me if I wanted to talk about it. I told him the whole story including the part about John and his mother coming over. Bob ran his hand through my hair and said "John you are going to have to learn to take some of this verbal abuse. It isn't just Indians that get it. I get called a 'squaw man' for marrying your mother. I have black friends that get called names, and a few white friends that get called a lot of things. The point is you just can't go around fighting everyone that is stupid.

This world is full of people that just don't think. Most people that are prejudice are trying to build up their own self-esteem. You will find that most prejudice people are lazy and uneducated.

Next time just look at them with disgust and walk away, believe me John fighting with them won't change them one bit. There is a lot of prejudice against the Indian, most of it is from a guilty conscience, for the way the whites stole this land from them so son be strong, work hard, and get a good education, don't fall into the trap the white man has set for you. Don't let the color of your skin be an excuse for failure."

Mom came out of the house, and Bob asked us if we wanted to go into town for dinner, Mom asked me where I wanted to go, and I said, "Mc Donald's. Bob laughed and said, "Well it's a good cheap place to eat." We jumped in his truck and drove to town.

When we went into Mc Donald's there was the other boy that I was in the fight with. His eye looked as bad as mine. I wanted to leave and told Bob that there was one of the boys I had fought with. He told Mom and me to go sit down. Then he walked over and talked to the man that was sitting with the boy. Bob looked over at me and told me to come over there. I was scared and didn't want to go, but I got up and walked over to the table. The man told me his name was Chuck and that his boys name was Charles. He shook hands with me and told Charles to apologize to me. We shook hands and I apologized to him also.

We went over and sat in the booth with Mom. I wasn't very hungry now; it upset me seeing this kid. I hadn't realized how much bigger than me he was. Mom asked me what I wanted to eat and I told her I wasn't hungry anymore; just seeing Charles had made me sick to my stomach and I was shaking inside. She ordered me a burger and a milkshake anyway. Charles and his dad left, and I started to feel better. I picked at the burger only eating about half of it, but I did drink all of the milkshake.

Bob could tell that I was upset, and tried to cheer me up. He said "John if you pick on them any bigger, you will have to bring a box to stand on just to reach their head." I laughed but it really wasn't funny. I asked Mom if I could go to Grandfathers tomorrow.

She said, "Yes John, I think a few days out there is what you need."

Bob drove me over to the reservation on his way to work. Grandfather was sitting on the front porch smoking his pipe and petting the old gray cat that was sitting in his lap. He took one look at my black eye, and just sat there smoking. After Bob left he asked, "What happened to your eye, John?" So I told him the story. He just grunted, and didn't say anything else. I got up and walked out to where Horse was. He came over to the fence and stuck his big nose right up to my sore eye. I pushed him away and said "Not you too!"

I got the fork and cleaned out the stall, then moved all the manure and straw out to a big pile behind the barn. Horse came in so I gave him a cup of grain and brushed him until he shined. I walked back to the porch and Grandfather was still sitting there; his pipe had gone out but he still held it in his mouth. He was about half asleep. I asked him if I could take my quest. He sat there for a few moments then pulled the pipe from his mouth, and said, "Two days." I asked about the snakes and wild animals. Grandfather said, "If you don't move they won't bother you. Then he asked, "John are you sure, that you're ready? This isn't a game! If you fail, this will follow you where ever you go."

I said, "Grandfather I am ready, and I won't fail. They call me Chief, remember?"

He lit his pipe and said "Two days".

I went into the house and gave Grandmother a big hug; of course I had to tell the whole story of my black eye again. If I ever get another black eye, I am going to write it down, and just give a copy to everyone I know, that way I won't have to keep explaining it, then I told Grandmother I was going to go ride Horse.

I took Horse out of the stall put the bridle and saddle pad on him, led him out the gate and mounted up. He wanted to run but I walked him until I was out of sight of the house, then I let him run; we were going out through the sagebrush and tumbleweeds as fast as Horse could go. I remembered the fall we had taken but I figured Horse would run like this even if I wasn't on him so I just sat low and let him run.

Horse was puffing pretty hard when we got to the river. I turned him loose and waded out into the water, and it was pretty cold. I could see some nice trout swimming in the riffles. I wished I had brought a fishing pole. Then I remembered the quest, so I walked over and sat on the bank and thought long and hard about the task I had ahead of me. Two things worried me; would I fail, and would I have a vision. I wanted an Indian name, a name that comes to you in a vision. Not copied from someone else, or one that you just dream up. I wanted a name that would command respect, not something that would brings a smile to peoples faces. Like my friend, "Sammy falls from his horse." This name fits Sammy well, and it's a good name, but it doesn't command respect. I will take the quest and see what the vision holds in store for me. The elders and the great spirits will lead me. "I will not fail."

CHAPTER VII

I had one more day before I did the quest. How could I prepare myself? I was afraid to ask any more questions of Grandfather. I was afraid he would tell me I wasn't ready.

I got up from the riverbank and caught Horse. I rode up into the rim rocks high above the reservation, as this was the place where I figured that I would take my quest. I tied Horse to a scrub juniper and walked out onto a rock shelf. I sat down here and looked out toward the valley below watching a hawk swoop down and back up only to repeat the process several times. My mind kept going back to the rattlesnake I had seen that day this worried me, as I don't like snakes. Could I sit and let one crawl over me?

I got up untied Horse and rode back to grandfathers'. Horse just walked slowly so I didn't hurry him I just rode and tried to vision what I had ahead of me. As Horse picked his way along through the sagebrush I was wishing that Sandy were they're holding me on. It wasn't likely that I would fall off I had learned to ride quite well. When we got home I put Horse in the stall grained, and rubbed him down good.

I walked out to the front porch where Grandfather was sitting picked up the old cat and petted him while he purred. Grandfather just sat there real quiet smoking his pipe, so I didn't say anything. My mind kept returning to the quest that lay before me. Tomorrow I would go to the river and really concentrate on what I am going to do.

I went to bed right after supper. I was up early and ate some cereal before Grandmother came into the kitchen. I told her I was going to ride down to the river, she told me to be careful and to come back early as I had to get ready for the next day. I walked out and got Horse, put the bridle and saddle pad on him. He was ready to run so I took out at a gallop. I let Horse pick his way and his own speed; he ran all the way to the river, walked out into the water splashing water with his front foot. I jumped into the water and swam for a few moments, than walked over to the bank by a large pine tree and sat down.

The sun was warm and the wet clothes I had on felt good. I sat there until I was almost asleep. Horse grazed along the riverbank, he raised his head when a deer walked out to get a drink. We both watched the deer for a while, and then he went on grazing. I lay back and dozed off. I don't know how long I had been dozing, when Horse snorted and started moving over to me. He stood there with his ears up snorting and looking toward the rock bluff beside the river.

A big mountain lion was sitting there looking at us. At first I was afraid, but I knew I could always go into the water and he probably wouldn't bother me there. I was more afraid for Horse than I was for myself. I was wishing I had my bow with me; I picked up some rocks and threw them at the big cat, and hollered real loud. The cat turned and ran but so did Horse. He took off running and bucking across the sagebrush until I could no longer see him. I really didn't want to walk all the way back across the high desert with a mountain lion hanging around.

I waited for nearly an hour and Horse never came back so I found me a good strong stick and started walking toward grandfathers' house. It was getting hot now and I was thirsty; I started cursing that stupid horse. I never hollered loud enough to scare him; sometimes that horse did things just to make me mad. The farther I walked the madder I got, I swore at that damn horse under my breath with each step I took. I suppose if the tribal leaders could see me now they would name me, 'John who can't find his Horse.'

It was a lot farther to walk than I realized, but I finally came in sight of grandfathers' house, and there was that dumb horse grazing on grandfathers' lawn. He came running when he saw me like I was going to grain him after he ran off. I turned him loose in the pasture without brushing him or giving him any grain.

I walked around to the porch and told Grandfather about seeing the lion. He said, "I wondered why Horse came back without you. He must have seen it too!"

I told him I hollered at the lion and scared Horse as well as the lion. Grandfather joked with me saying, "We can call you, 'John No Horse'. That way you won't have to earn a tribal name." He tapped the ashes out of his pipe and went into the house. I put the old cat down, and walked out to Horses pen to clean the stall, and scoop up the poop in front of the barn. Horse came in so I gave him some grain brushed his coat real good and cleaned his hoofs with a pick, and checked him all over for ticks. I tried to look at his ears but he sure didn't like me messing with them. I should have kicked his behind for making me walk back. Grandfather came out and stood by the fence.

He said, "John don't fail me or yourself tomorrow. Stick it out no matter what happens. You have asked to do this. "Just remember that."

I thought for a moment then looked into his black eyes, and said, "They call me Chief, and no chief I ever knew has failed himself or his people."

Grandfather reached out and put his arm around me. "We will see!" He said, "We will see!"

We went into the house and Grandfather called me into his bedroom. He reached into a closet and brought out a pair of buckskin breeches, a blue loincloth and a red cloth headband. He said, "You will wear these tomorrow: men of this family before have worn them. Do not be the first to dishonor them." He also gave me a bear claw necklace with several large beads on it. "These you will keep and pass them on to your son, or grandson, when his time of manhood shall come."

I took the clothes to the room I was sleeping in, and placed them on the foot of the bed. I took my beaded moccasins from my pack, and lay them with the clothes. I would wear no shirt, but have a blanket given to me by Grandmother for the occasion. Now all I could do was wait for morning. I ate very little for dinner and didn't drink anything after that. I went to bed early and tried to think about what tomorrow would bring.

The next thing I knew, Grandfather was shaking me and saying; "John it is time". It was still dark out, but I could hear several people talking in the other room. I put on the buckskin breeches and the loincloth plus the red headband. I neatly folded the blanket and carried it over my left arm. I had almost forgotten the necklace; I put it on and looked in the mirror. There stood a scared Indian boy looking back at me. I thought: would an Indian man be looking back after this is over?

I walked into the other room and was greeted by several Indian men all decked out in ceremonial dress. This was the first time I had seen Grandfather wear traditional Indian clothing. I only knew Mr. Fox and the tribal medicine man, the others I hadn't seen before. There were eight men including my grandfather. We got into four pickups and drove for what seemed like hours. The sun was up when we stopped on an old road that was grown over by little trees.

Everyone got out and we walked about a mile up a winding path through tall trees to a clearing on the edge of a high bluff. There was a large flat rocky outcropping near the edge that overlooked a beautiful valley below that stretched out for miles. I had never been here before. I was led over to the rock and told that this was the place I would seek my vision. A blanket was folded and placed on the rock for me to sit on.

Bunches of sweet grass were lighted and the smoke blown over my body to purify me. Black Eagle the medicine man placed a string around my neck that had dried fruit looking things on it. I was told to chew on them if I got real thirsty. The other elders were beating small drums, and chanting a song that I had heard many times before at other ceremonies. Black Eagle told me to sit here, and to stay here until he returned the next day. The drumming got louder and my heart beat harder. Then all was quiet. I wanted to turn around and look. Were they all still there watching me? I hadn't heard anyone leave or any car door shut.

The sun was now straight overhead I could see the shadows of the weeds as small as they would get. I picked out a stick in front of me and watched its shadow, this way I could track time for a while. All I had was a blanket beside me and the one I was sitting on, plus a coup stick that one of the elders had given me just before he left.

The coup stick was covered in places with rawhide shrunken real tight, there were three eagle feathers, and some owl feathers tied to it, plus the top was bent over and the hair from a horses tail was glued to it. The stick was shiny and worn like it had been handled many times. The sun got hotter as the afternoon wore on. I was wondering if I was getting sunburned or not. I had been in the sun a lot but not sitting still. The shadow under the stick was getting longer and pointing away from me.

Soon the sun would be setting lower, and hitting me in the back. I was facing east, so that the morning sun would be in my face and I could see the new day come alive. I was already hot and thirsty and I probably hadn't been there over two hours.

I prayed to the Great Father to get me through this. Beads of sweat ran down over my nose and into my eyes. I was hot, thirsty, and hungry, but the day was just getting started. I looked at the heavens above me and watched clouds float across the blue sky. How would I know a vision if I had one? I wasn't told much about all of this. I sat and watched everything that moved, every little bird that flew past, and the insects that crawled on and past me. I watched a small rabbit hop from bush to bush, looking for something green to eat.

As the sun grew warmer on my back I shut my eyes and drifted off into a light sleep. I would awaken a little each time my head dropped only to doze off again; finally I was in a deep sleep. I was dreaming of Horse and the river I wanted to go for a swim and Horse kept me from the water. I was cursing him and trying to push him away; I awoke and it was nearly dark. The shadow of the stick was completely gone, and the air was getting cooler. I heard a rustle in the bushes beside me and a spotted skunk come nosing out of the brush followed by two smaller ones.

I thought: this is just great, here I will be called, 'Boy Who Stink like Skunk'. I sat motionless, as they got closer. The larger one stomped its feet at me, and stood on its front feet. I shut my eyes and waited for the spray, finally I opened one eye and they had gone past and into the brush. As it got darker I could see several deer moving from the brush going down to a green spot where I figured there must be a water hole. I watched this spot as long as I could see. Animals of all kinds kept coming down to it. I watched two badgers fight each other all the way to the green spot, and later they came out still fighting as they went on their way. I figured they must be mates.

Darkness overcame me and for a while I couldn't see anything. I pulled my blanket tight over my shoulders as the cool air blew across the ridge. Soon the coyotes were howling all around me, at times they sounded like they were right behind me. I was starting to get a little bit scared. I didn't like the dark. I felt something pass over my head like a large bird. It must have been an owl, as they fly quietly.

I shut my eyes and tried to sleep some more, but the night sounds kept coming. I could hear the wind in the trees up the mountain and hear the rustle of the sagebrush as the wind blew through it. I could hear something sniffing the air behind me. I wanted to turn around so bad but I sat perfectly still. I could hear footsteps and twigs breaking and a low growl. I knew if I turned I had failed so I made up my mind if something attacked me then I would fight, until then I would sit tight.

Then everything got perfectly quiet, I couldn't hear a bug, frogs or anything only the total stillness of the night. It was so quiet that it almost hurt to listen to it. I looked up and there were a million stars shining down. I thought is there life up there someplace? And are other boys doing the same thing as me? There was a crashing sound high on the mountain; I almost jumped off the rock. Then it was totally quiet again, I think a tree must have fallen.

Soon I heard the chirping of a single frog down by the water hole, then another frog, and soon it was real noisy, as hundreds of frogs and crickets were singing and I could hear the cooing of a night bird. Again a large bird flew past my head on silent wings. I hoped an owl didn't grab my head thinking I was a small animal. The coyote's started up again, and soon they were howling all around me.

It got totally quiet again just like a switch had been shut off. I strained to hear something. It was like I had gone deaf. I snapped my fingers to see if I was hearing. After a few moments the frogs and bugs started up their night songs again, and I could hear larger animals jumping through the brush around me. A deer snorted after catching my scent; the sound made me jump. Soon the moon came over the ridge, it was only about a half moon but it did lighten things up some.

I wondered if the elders and Grandfather were watching me. Surely someone would stay to see if I violated the trust they had put in me. How would they know if I moved or turned around? I would know, and that would be enough. I now realized how much this put on me. I would not fail.

The thirst was really getting bad all I could think of was the cool water that was probably oozing out of the ground at the green spot below me I figured I had been there for ten to twelve hours so I would be half through the quest. I was tempted to turn my head and look around, but I held true to the trust that had been laid on me. I must prove myself to the elders and to my own self I would know if I cheated, or didn't do as instructed. I would be the one who had to live with this the rest of my life. I would not shame my family, my people, or myself.

I was jarred out of my thoughts by a crashing sound with the pounding of hoofs that sounded like a horse running toward me. I sat motionless listening to the sound as it came closer, and closer, would I be overrun by a large animal? A large bull elk came running out of the trees, and ran within inches of me. I wanted to duck or move but I sat quietly and didn't turn my head. All was quiet again, had this really happened? Or was I having hallucinations. Did I really see what I thought I saw? It was very dark with shadows cast by the half moon that was low on the horizon. I tried to sleep again my head dropped, and woke me up each time I dozed off, but soon I was in a deep sleep dreaming of water a huge lake of water, I wanted to drink from it but there were dead fish floating in it. I could smell the putrid odor of them all about me.

All of a sudden I was awake something was behind me, smelling of me, its breath was putrid, and I guess that is why I dreamed of the dead fish, this thing smelled like rotten fish. I could feel its hot breath as it breathed on me. I wanted to turn, to jump up and run. Every nerve and muscle in my body was tense and ready for flight. Was this for real or were the elders testing me. I sat motionless barely breathing. I felt the thing touch my shoulder, and then it jumped back and snorted. I couldn't help but jump, and then I could see this huge black shadow coming around my left side. I strained my eye trying to look to the left as far as I could without turning my head.

The moon became obstructed behind a cloud; it was now too dark to see it. I could still smell the animal, but I couldn't hear any movement. I thought about lashing out with the coup stick, but I remembered what Grandfather had said 'If I sat motionless nothing would bother me.' Besides I was now too scared to move. My heart was pounding in my chest, I lost all craving for food or water, my body no longer cramped from the position I had been sitting in.

I prayed to the Great Father the creator of the universe, and creator of everything that dwelled upon it. I prayed for strength and guidance that nothing would stop me from this quest.

Where were the elders? Was Grandfather near enough to help me if I called out? Was Black Eagle watching me from afar? Or was I alone here on this mountain in the ancient burial places of my people. This animal that smelled so bad was it real or was I seeing and feeling something that wasn't really there?

Soon the clouds passed by the moon, and I could see the huge shadow swaying back and forth beside me. I could still smell the putrid odor of rotten fish and the smell of a wet dog. Suddenly something licked the side of my face, I ducked and nearly jumped from the blanket, a huge dog jumped back and barked in my face. My heart was screaming and every nerve in my body exploded. I struck out with the coup stick and the dog yelped as I hit him. He stood there and growled at me. I sat with the stick ready to strike him again then he slowly turned and slunk off into the brush. Then I remembered seeing a large wild dog down by the river one day, a huge, wolf-like dog that was eating dead salmon.

I was really scared by this ordeal. I sat there and shook from the tenseness and fear, as well as the cold. I sat and listened for a long time. The moon went below the horizon and now it was total darkness. All of the frogs and bugs had quit chirping, I could hear a cow bawling in the far off distance, and then all was quiet. My mouth was now so dry I couldn't swallow and my stomach churned with hunger from the adrenalin pumped into it by the dog scare. Every muscle in my body ached, I wanted to stand up to stretch my muscles and move my joints.

My mouth was drying out so bad now that my tongue was starting to swell. I remembered the dried fruit like things that Black Eagle had placed around my neck. I reached up and pulled it close to my mouth and bit off a small piece.

It was hard and rubbery to chew; I sucked on it for a while until a little saliva formed in my mouth. Now I could chew it better it tasted bitter, but it made more saliva form in my mouth so I bit off another small piece, and chewed it for a long time before swallowing the juice from it. My heart was still pounding from the ordeal with the dog my body felt weak, and I was shaking was it from the cold or the scare I had just had?

My tongue was getting thicker and I had a vile taste in my mouth from the fruit I had chewed. I was getting nauseas, and felt like throwing up. I was sweating heavily yet I was cold. The world around me was starting to spin and I was getting very dizzy, the stars would no longer stay in place, they danced all about the heavens and I could see some light forming in the east. Then a dark cloud loomed in front of me. I could see the faces of animals looking out from it, a snarling badger, a wolf, and the mountain lion. I closed my eyes and everything went dark.

CHAPTER VIII

With the darkness came a bitter cold, I was shaking violently as I sat there with my head spinning, and the stars were going in circles while bright shards of lights were streaking by me from the east. I became sick to my stomach, and was trying to heave but nothing was coming up. All the time that large cloud full of snarling animals was getting closer, and closer, I could hear someone screaming.

My head was roaring and throbbing, I could feel and hear each heart beat as it pounded in my chest. The cloud was getting closer, I couldn't move, I was frozen in place my legs and arms wouldn't work, and the screaming was getting louder. Then I realized it was me who was screaming. Suddenly a giant bear came charging at me from the center of the cloud, his gaping mouth wide-open and large fangs dripping with saliva.

I tried to jump and run, but my whole body was paralyzed. I could hear myself screaming again but I couldn't stop. Just as the huge bear got to me he split in half, and became two bears one racing past me on each side only to turn and go back into the cloud. I could hear the screaming of a giant eagle as a dark shadow passed over me. The noise from the animals growling and barking was so loud my ears ached. Once again the huge bear again tore from the cloud and came directly at me with his mouth wide open ready to swallow me; as the gaping mouth engulfed me it again turned into two bears and went streaking past me like two wisps of smoke.

From atop the cloud stood an Indian warrior dressed in buckskin and beads. He stood there holding a large war shield and lance that was strung with eagle feathers. He stood there looking down at me his face held no expression; his eyes were as piercing as an arrow, yet I showed no fear from him. Beside him stood two giant bears, only one bear had the face of my father; the other bear had a face I did not recognize. I studied it for a long time; finally I realized it was my own face. The giant warrior stood there looking at me, it was like he was looking clear through me searching my soul. Finally he waved his lance and the cloud vanished; now the sky was filled with bright lights, so bright I couldn't open my eyes.

I could hear the chanting of a medicine man and the beating of a drum. I became sicker and sicker. My mouth was so dry I couldn't swallow or speak. My whole body was shaking so hard I couldn't control it. Pain shot through my body like a thousand needles I was screaming again. Then everything was quiet. It was dark and I was lying down on the rock. I could no longer sit up. I became conscious of a cool wet liquid being poured slowly over my face and head. I opened my mouth and let the cool fluid enter my body; I had a hard time trying to swallow it.

I opened my eyes and the sun was straight over me. Someone was holding onto me, I tried to rise up, but I couldn't find the strength, everything went dark again now I was laying on cool green grass while Horse stood over me. He was drooling onto my face I tried to push him away, and then he turned into the wild dog I had seen, it too was slobbering and dripping into my mouth. I tried to spit, but my tongue wouldn't work. I became choked and started coughing; I was gagging and trying to throw up. All the time strong hands held me.

I could hear voices; that of my grandfather calling my name. "John!" He said, "Johnny can you hear me?" I tried to speak but no sound would come, all I could do was to make a gurgling sound. I raised my hand up and felt the strong grip of Grandfather as he took my hand. I held on tightly to him, I tried to sit up but the big dog kept licking my face, and drooling in my mouth, each time I tried to spit and became violently sick. The light was too bright and painful to look at; all I could see were images of people standing and kneeling about me. The cool liquid kept running down my face. In my unconscious state I finally realized that someone was pouring water on me and wiping my face with a wet cloth. What I had envisioned as the wild dog drooling on me was actually the trickle of water they were pouring on me.

I had gone without water, sitting in the hot sun, for over thirty hours. I was severely dehydrated. I reached out and took the water bag and drank a long hard drink, only to throw it all back up again. I felt better this time and my eyes were starting to focus. Again Black Eagle told me to drink, but too do it more slowly this time. He gave me a green plant to chew on. It tasted bitter like the stem of a dandelion, and I am sure that was what it was.

Grandfather knelt beside me and held me in his arms, he said, "It's all over now John. You are now truly a man, ready to take your place in the tribal society of warriors. Now you must tell us of the things you envisioned." I tried to talk, my voice sounded funny, I had a hard time forming words, my throat was sore and my tongue was still thick.

Gradually I told them of the great cloud, filled with snarling animals that came past me, of the great bear that lunged at me and split into two bears, only to return to the cloud and do the same thing again. And of the great warrior who stood with piercing eyes, and how he looked at me and about the bears with my face and that of my father. And of the decorated lance and shield held by him, and the painted facial markings he wore.

I told them of how I felt at peace in the presence of such a warrior. Black Eagle and the others sat and looked at each other for a long time. Finally Grandfather spoke, "He has seen the Great One, the Chief of all warriors, the leader of those who have long since fallen in battle. This is a good sign, 'Johnny Two Bears' you will grow strong, and someday you will lead our people. They will call you Chief."

I was helped to my feet, my legs were so cramped I couldn't stand alone. Grandfather helped me; he walked me around and back up to the place I had sat. Together we looked out over the valley, where I had sat and stared for over thirty hours, a place where a vision cloud overcame me. I could see the pride in my grandfather's eyes, and face. He had brought a boy to this place and transformed him into a man. I had completed the vision quest, and gotten the name of 'Two Bears' it was a good name, a name to command honor when spoken. A name I shall always wear with honor, I will not shame it or my people. I am "Johnny Two Bears."

Suddenly I felt different; I looked at the elders and Grandfather with much more respect. These men had all gone through a quest such as me. I don't know if all of them had a vision or not. It does not matter, as long as they go through the quest for a vision. I still feel that I am destined to lead my people. I will prepare myself in every way I can, I will learn the white mans law as it pertains to the Indian people. Much has been taken from us. I must work hard in school and get a good education.

I became sick again and Grandfather walked me back down the trail to the truck. We sat there on the tailgate of the truck and drank water until I was sick of it. I poured water over my head, and then I realized I was really sun burned. I was a true red skin, and my back and arms felt red hot and looked worse. Black Eagle rubbed some sap from a vine all over me; it felt cool and soothing. I then walked down the lane on trembling legs but I was getting stronger. I wanted to talk with Grandfather about the things I had seen, both in my vision and before, especially about the great elk that had almost run over me.

I walked back to the truck and sat with Grandfather and the others. Black Eagle said, "Johnny Two Bears, you have been through a vision that many never attempt. You have honored yourself, your family, and your people. This thing you have done is very sacred; it must not be talked about except in council, or with others that have passed this way. It is better that others walk their own path and seek out their own visions. You are only one of a few who have seen the 'Great Warrior', he will be with you always, and in times of trouble he will come and it will help you through. Much strength will come, both physical and mental from what you have been through."

Even though you are a young man, you have now earned the right to sit in council with all the tribal leaders, and this I encourage you to do. Study the ways of your people and the ways of the whites. By doing this you can be a leader of all races, we are many races of people but under the 'Great One' we are all his children. Go! Johnny Two Bears and keep your mind and body strong. When the world calls on you, be ready to lead, our nation needs strong leaders."

I sat quietly through the ride home, many things went through my mind, things that I didn't understand and maybe never will. When we arrived home Grandmother was waiting for us. She never looked directly at me but down at the ground. I ran over and gave her a hug. She ran her hand through my hair and said, "John you need a bath" After all I had been through it was like Grandmother to clean me up. I ran bath water in the tub and soaked for a long time, it felt good to be clean of both body and spirit. Grandmother took the breeches and loincloth, to clean them for me. Grandfather took the necklace and headband and said he would store everything until I had a home of my own.

I suddenly realized I was starving. My stomach was empty except for the water I had drunk. Grandmother fixed me a snack, and I walked out onto the porch, sat and held the old gray cat while I ate. When I had finished it I took my plate back to the kitchen and walked out back to see Horse. He stood in the middle of the pasture and looked at me with his ears up like he was looking at a total stranger. I called to him and he came running over to the fence.

His stall needed cleaning so I gave him some grain to keep him out of my way. I cleaned the stall and all the manure that was in front of the barn.

I brushed Horse until he shined in the sun. Then I jumped on him without any bridle or saddle pad. He took off running around the pasture as I held tightly with my legs. I sure didn't want to fall off, and have to take another bath, so when he slowed down I jumped off. I was getting very tired so I went in and lay down on grandmother's couch.

I must have fallen asleep instantly. I was dreaming of a huge blue elk that kept trying to step on me. I would push him away and he would turn into Horse. Then I dreamed of the wild dog, I had seen in my vision. Was he really a vision or had he actually been there? I kept dreaming dream after dream, most of them silly things, bears with eagle heads and badgers that could fly. Suddenly I jumped and was wide-awake. I went back to sleep and when I awoke it was dark out. I got up and went into my bedroom and crawled in bed, when I awoke it was late in the day. I had slept for many hours. It was almost lunchtime and I was ready. Grandmother must have known I would be hungry for she had fixed a big lunch and baked a hot apple pie. I loved grandmother's pies, she was the best cook in the entire world, and I told her so, especially every time she made a pie.

After lunch I went back out on the porch where Grandfather sat smoking his pipe. This time he talked to me more than he ever had before. I told him about the great blue elk that had almost run over me on the mountain. He smiled and a light came into his eyes, "Did you really see that John?" he asked.

I said "I seen it, I felt it, and I heard it." I also told him about the wild dog that licked my face, and about the wild dog I had seen one day down on the river. That I believed it was the same one. He smiled and said, "You should have told us about this on the mountain. We could have named you wild dog, instead of Two Bears." He sort of chuckled.

This made me feel good, for I had not seen Grandfather laugh many times. I felt closer to him now than I ever had. I wanted to tell him how much I cared for him, but I was ashamed to put it in words. This I could not understand, why if we really love someone can't we tell him or her? Are we afraid they don't feel the same way toward us? I had wanted to tell my father goodbye, and that I loved him that day at the cemetery, but I just kept silent. I am sure he knew without me saying it. But why should I be afraid to say it?

I got up and walked over and put my arms around Grandfather and said, "Grandfather I love you very much. I want to thank you for all the things you do for me. I am truly blessed to have grandparents like you and Grandmother." He reached up and patted me on the arm, stood up and walked out toward the back of the house. I could see tears running down his darkened cheeks. Had I embarrassed him? Or were these just tears of emotional happiness. Finally he turned around and with tears still running down his face said. "Thank you Johnny. Some day they will truly call you, 'Chief'. Now get out of here and go see if you can find that wild dog. Take something to feed him and don't try to get too close until he gets used to you."

I felt good inside as I walked out and caught Horse. I put the bridle on him and left the saddle pad in the barn. I swung up on his back, kicked him with my heels and we left the pasture on a dead run. It felt good to be on Horse again, the desert air was fresh and clear. I let Horse pick his way through the deer brush and sage. He loved to run. I sat far forward to be over his front legs, this seemed to give him more power when he jumped over sage and other brush. We went all the way to the river before Horse slowed down, and then walked out into the water. He was puffing so hard he couldn't drink, so he just stood there and pawed at the water with his front foot.

After Horse drank his fill I rode him up river for several miles than circled back toward the high desert. I was looking for the stray dog. I saw a couple of coyotes and a huge bobcat. After a couple of miles we had turned back toward the river, when I saw the big dog on a ridge far above me. He was going toward the river. As soon as he dropped out of sight I kneed Horse into a run and headed for the draw that led to the bottom of the ridge. As we got close to where the ridge sloped down toward the river I slowed Horse to a walk. I walked him real slow, and as we came in sight of the river, there stood the big dog looking at me about a hundred yards away. I wish I had done like Grandfather said and brought something to feed him.

I sat real still and talked softly to the dog. He stood and watched me, not moving a muscle. I whistled to him and his ears came up. I kneed Horse and walked him closer to the large dog, talking softly all the time. He let me get within about twenty yards of him before he turned and ran off a few steps. I got off Horse and sat down, and started calling to him. He came a few steps toward me than walked toward the side of me. I kept talking to him all the time. Finally he just sat down and watched me with those pointed ears listening for every sound.

This wasn't truly a wild dog. I could tell by his actions he had been around people. I think he was just lost out here. I lay down and watched him; he stood up and came a few steps closer to me. I held out my hand and called to him. He watched me for a long time but wouldn't come any closer. I got up and walked over and jumped on Horse, and rode off calling him. I was really surprised that he followed me. I rode slow talking to him all the time. Once he came up almost beside me.

As we got close to grandfathers house, he turned and loped off into the desert. I put Horse in the stall, brushed him down made sure he had clean water, then I went into the house and asked Grandmother for some bread, or meat scraps that I could put out for the dog. I walked out to the end of the pasture and put the scraps under a bush, hoping the magpies wouldn't steal them. I stayed and watched for a while but nothing came, so I walked back to the house, and went around to the front porch and played with the old cat while I told Grandfather about the dog.

I asked Grandfather if I could keep the dog if I could get him to come to me. He said, "John, if he wants to come here, he is welcome, we won't tie him up. If he wants to be with you he will stay and be welcome, as long as he doesn't get into trouble, killing someone's chickens or sheep, if that happens he will have to be destroyed. So don't get too attached to him until you find out how wild he may be."

Mother came over to get me the next day, and I had to go back to town and mow the yard and do some more painting for Bob. I wanted to go see Sandy anyway, so I was eager to go when Mom showed up. She stayed and visited with Grandmother for a while. As we were driving away she turned toward me and said, "So, Two Bears, I hear you had a little excitement in your life."

I said, "It was interesting and exciting, plus a whole lot scary".

"Well!" she said, "We are all very proud of you." I sat there in silence wondering how much she knew about the quest. I didn't believe that women did such things. I know, as young Indian girls become women, they spent time in some sort of a ceremonial lodge with the older women of the tribe, so I guess they go through a rite of some kind.

I had just gotten started mowing the yard when Sandy rode up on her bicycle, so I shut the mower off and walked over and sat on the porch with her. She looked at me then said, "So! Did you get your Indian name?" This kind of embarrassed me; I couldn't remember telling her about going for my quest. So I asked her how she knew about that, and she said that she had been over and talked with my Mom one day while I was gone.

"Yes!" I said, "It is Boy who gets eye blacked."

She said, "Boy going to get other eye blacked if he don't wise up". We both laughed and I told her, it was 'Two Bears', then she wanted to know why I got that name, so I told her that was what the elders gave me. Then she wanted to know all about that thing I was supposed to go through. I made the mistake of saying that it was sacred and I couldn't talk about it. I should have known better, she got all huffy, and got up and rode off on her bike. So I took it out on the lawn mower. I bet that is the fastest that lawn ever got mowed. I got out the paint and started painting on the shed. I wrote Sandy on the side of the building, and drew an ugly face with the paintbrush. Yep! You guessed it; here came Sandy and Jill on their bikes. You never saw anyone sling paint as fast as I did, only I wasn't fast enough; they had seen it from up the street.

I never sweated this much during the whole quest. Sandy asked me about the picture, and why I painted it out. I thought fast and I told her, that I couldn't draw her beautiful hair with this type of a paintbrush, so I just painted over it. This really caught her off guard, and I could see then that I had won this round. She just stood there and stuttered, with her mouth open, while Jill giggled.

CHAPTER IX

Sandy got on her bike and rode off. Jill was still looking over her shoulder at me and laughing. I had learned something here about the fairer sex, if you pay them a compliment in the heat of an argument; they loose all sense of control. Or I think they do; only time will tell. I will have to test this theory some more. I finished painting the shed and done some weeding around the house.

I asked Mom if I could ride my bike down to the park, and she said ok, after a three-minute lecture about fighting; heck I still had one black eye I sure didn't want another one. Big Larry and another kid named Joe were there shooting baskets so I played with them for a while. Sandy never showed up so I rode over by her house. She and Jill were sitting out on the porch so I rode up and stopped. She said, "Well if it isn't the artist!"

I said, "I sure wish I was, so I could capture all of your beauty on canvas, Jill about spit out her gum laughing, but Sandy just turned beet red and stuttered some more. So far my theory was working.

I looked at Sandy and grinned, she was trying to think of something to say so I beat her to it. I asked her when she wanted to go ride horses again.

She said, "I will have to ask Mom, my father doesn't like for me to go out there, on the reservation with you. He doesn't think it is safe out there, with all those wild Indians." Then she smiled; now I was on the defense, and didn't have an answer. So I just smiled and said, "I am the only wild Indian out there!" She said, "Yes I know and I think you are the one he is afraid of. But I will ask Mom if we can go tomorrow, if that is ok?" I told her I would have to see if Bob could take us, and we might have to ride Horse double, unless I can borrow Jake again, and he doesn't go lame on us. She smiled and said, "Bet you would like that!" We both laughed. I told her I would call her later, and see if everything was all right to go.

Mom said that she would take us over, as she wanted to visit with Grandmother. It was ok so I called Sandy and my mom talked to her mom and everything was settled. I did some more work around the yard pulling weeds and trimming, cleaning up everything I could find. I didn't want Bob telling me I had a lot of things to do before I could go. I even washed mom's car for her.

I went to bed early, and got up early. I had already eaten a bowl of cereal before Mom and Bob got up. He teased me, saying, "You are a little eager this morning. That Sandy must be some girl." I just smiled and didn't say anything. We left for Sandy's house shortly after Bob left for work. Mom went in, and visited with her mother while Sandy and I sat on the porch and talked.

When we got to the reservation I asked Mom to drop me off at Mr. Fox's house so we could borrow a horse. Mr. Fox was glad to see us. We talked to him and Mrs. Fox for a little while, and I asked him if we could ride Jake again. We walked out back picked up a feed bucket and banged it on the fence and several horses came running. I caught Jake and put a bridle and saddle pad on him. I led Jake out of the corral and jumped up on his back. Sandy stood on the corral fence and got on behind me.

She said, "You had this all planned, so that I would have to ride with you. Didn't you?" I said, "Yep, me pretty smart injun" We both laughed and she squeezed me tight, then I thought I am a pretty smart injun. We rode over to grandfather's house. Horse was at the fence looking at us. I caught him, and put a saddle pad and halter on him. I asked Sandy which horse she wanted to ride. She decided to stay on Jake. I told Mom we were going to ride down by the river and look for the wild dog again.

We got the customary be careful lecture, and rode off.

We let the horses run for a while; Sandy seemed to be handling Jake ok, so we let them pick their own speed. It was a beautiful day on the high desert. We rode up onto the rock bluff overlooking the river, and I took Sandy over to the spot where I had found the bees.

I showed her the opening to the cave that I had piled rocks over, and told her about the human bones I had found, and about the bees. There were still a few bees coming and going through the small opening. Horse didn't like this place and still wanted to run off. We rode downriver for several miles to a big meadow that was grown over by reeds; it was pretty swampy in there so we rode around it, watching all the nesting ducks and geese. We rode back over to a small lake and got off the horses and walked along the edge of the lake looking for arrowheads.

I took off my belt twisted it and made some hobbles to put on Jake, so we could catch him. I should let him wander off, and then we both would have to ride back on one horse. We left the horses to graze along the lake. I picked some wild flowers and made a bouquet for Sandy; she gave me a hug and a peck on the cheek as she thanked me. We had walked a lot farther around the lake then I had noticed. I could no longer see the horses, and decided we had better get back to where we could watch them.

Suddenly I could hear a screaming sound and a horse whinny. The noise got louder. I told Sandy to come on, and I ran toward the horses. I could see Jake floundering around in the reeds with Horse nowhere to be seen. As I got nearer I saw a large mountain lion jump on Jake. He was squealing, kicking, and floundering around in the mud. The hobbles I put on him weren't helping him any. I picked up a dead stick and ran at the big cat hollering as loud as I could. The lion turned and came at me. I stood there screaming and waving the stick, as the lion started to circle toward where Sandy was. Jake had now fallen over on his side and was kicking and fighting to get up in the mud. The hobbles were tangled in the reeds and he couldn't get his feet under him.

I wanted to get the hobbles off of him, but the big cat was now looking at Sandy and was between us. I was afraid it would attack her. I moved back to try and get between them; the lion was screaming and growling at me. I moved toward the lion, and it crouched to jump at me. I didn't have a knife, just the stick I had picked up and it wasn't that big. I wanted to tell Sandy to run, but I was afraid the lion would go after her. Jake was still floundering around on his side in the mud his front feet hopelessly tangled in the reeds, and my belt. I told Sandy to back up real slow, and to get in the water, and if the lion came at her, to go out as deep as she could.

I started shouting and swinging the stick from side to side as fast as I could, while waving my other arm. The lion just sat there and snarled at me as I moved to my left to get between the lion and Sandy. The lion stood up and came a couple steps closer to me; it was snarling and striking out with its front feet. I could see the razor sharp claws, fully extended. I could hear something behind me but I was afraid to turn and look, maybe Horse had come back.

I heard a growl, and a huge gray form shot past me. All I could see was a big gray ball of hair landing in the middle of the lion. Then I realized that it was the wild dog. I ran to where Jake was tangled up, loosened my belt and held on tight to his halter. He lunged to his feet and dragged me from the swamp still holding on . I had a hard time holding onto him. The dog and lion were still fighting in the reeds; the dog was growling, and barking and the lion was screaming, along with Sandy who was really scared by now.

Jake was dragging me all over the place; he had stepped on me twice, and my foot felt like it was broken. Suddenly the dog yelped and the lion tore out of the reeds heading for the high rocky cliffs nearby. I finally got Jake calmed down enough so that I thought Sandy could hold him. She was crying and shaking really bad. I stood there and held her and told her everything was ok. Jake was still pretty scared and he kept jumping around. I could see Horse walking toward us real slow with his ears and tail held straight up. He was really scared too, and I wasn't the bravest Indian on the reservation at this time.

I looked over and the big dog was lying there in the mud bleeding. I caught Horse and tied him and Jake to a nearby tree, hoping they wouldn't get spooked and break loose on me. I walked over to the big dog; he growled real low in his throat and then made a whimpering sound. I slowly reached down so he could smell my hand, then I rubbed his head. He tried to stand; he had several deep cuts on his neck and shoulders. I couldn't see any really bad wounds, but he wouldn't put any weight on his front leg, and when I felt it he yelped. He got up and hobbled down to the lake and drank some water. Then he lay down in the water and just stayed there.

I walked over to where the horses were tied. I put both arms around Sandy and she said she was ok. I stood there and held her tight; I could feel her heart pounding in her chest. I kissed her on top of the head and told her I was sorry about all of this. I had forgotten about seeing the lion here before. I never thought he would go after the horses. But with Jake hobbling around with my belt on both front legs, he probably looked like a crippled animal to the lion, and easy prey. As I looked over at the horses, I could see streaks of blood on Jake so I untied him and walked him out into the lake and started washing some of the mud off of him.

Sandy waded out into the lake and helped me wash Jake. He had several deep scratches on his rear end and a deep bite mark on his neck. We cleaned up Jake the best we could. I told Sandy we had better take him back to Mr. Fox and get him doctored up. I helped her up onto Jake and then got on Horse; as we rode off the big dog hobbled along beside us. We rode slow and easy all the way back. Sandy was worried that her mom wouldn't let her come riding anymore if she found out what happened.

I rode up beside her and said, "Don't you think you should ride double with me, and let Jake rest being that he is injured?" She laughed and got onto Horse behind me. She put both arms around me and put her head on my back and squeezed me real tight. She said, "Chief, I was really scared back there but you stood your ground, wasn't you scared of that lion?" I said, "Yes, but I was a little too busy to think of it. I don't know what would have happened if that dog hadn't showed up."

We looked down at the big dog and he was now walking on all four feet, so he didn't appear to be too badly hurt. Then I thought of my foot that Jake had stomped on, I looked down and moved it around, and it seemed to be ok. When we got to grandfathers house we were both pretty dirty. My mom wanted to know if we had fallen into the river. She made Sandy go in and take a bath while she washed her clothes, saying; "girl I can't take you home looking like that".

Grandfather came out and looked at Jake and decided that he wasn't hurt too badly. Then he looked at the big dog that was lying in the shade of the barn. "Is that the wild dog you've been telling me about?"

I told Grandfather the whole story about the dog fighting the lion. We walked over and the dog got up and shied away from Grandfather. I caught him and held him while Grandfather came over; the dog growled at Grandfather at first then settled down. Grandfather looked him over and said: "He isn't hurt much but we will put some liniment on those cuts if he will let us. Then you better take Mr. Fox's horse back to him and see if he wants a vet, to look at him."

We put some of the horse liniment on the dog's cuts; he growled a little at first then stood still and let us doctor him. I went into the house and got some bread to feed him, then I gave him a bucket of fresh water and he lay back down in the shade. I took Mr. Fox's horse back to him. He smeared some suave on the scratches and looked at the bite marks on Jake and decided he would be ok. I apologized for getting him hurt but Mr. Fox just laughed and said, "Two Bears any time you want one of my horses you come and get him. I know you will treat them right. We will have to hunt that lion down and kill him, or he will attack another horse, now that he has started." I thanked Mr. Fox and started to run home, only my foot hurt so bad I couldn't run on it.

When I got back to grandfathers house, Grandmother had lunch fixed for us and Sandy was sitting wrapped up in one of grandmother's robes, with her hair all wet. I called her granny and that didn't go over too good. I had to go take a bath before I could eat, and Mom washed my clothes. Luckily I had a change of clothes to put on. While I was in the bath I noticed that my foot was swelling real bad and black on top. I put clean socks on and didn't say anything. I was hungry and ready to eat; I didn't have time to worry about a sore foot.

I told the whole story of the lion attack again while we ate. I left out all the heroics, about how I had fought the lion with only a little stick. I was hoping that Sandy would speak up and glorify me a little. She just sat there stuffing her face and smiling at me.

Mom asked if I was scared, which embarrassed me so I said, "Well if I could have gotten to Jake I would have rode for help, and let Sandy fight that old lion." We all laughed. Later I found out Sandy had told them all about it while I was taking a bath.

Sandy asked if we had to tell her folks about all this.

Mom said "Yes I think we should. I believe they will understand, this is just one of those things that happens, and no one got hurt, even though it was a dangerous situation. Next time you will have to ride closer to home, and I don't believe that lion would have attacked Jake had he not been hobbled. I will explain everything to Sandy's folks when we get her home."

My foot was really hurting bad, but I put my shoe on it anyway and tried to walk without limping. After lunch Mom and Sandy helped

Grandmother with the dishes and I sat out on the porch with Grandfather and the cat. Then I thought about the dog and walked around the house and called to him, when he came around to the porch; the old gray cat climbed on top of grandfather's shoulders and started hissing at the dog.

The dog lay down by the steps and I petted him. Pretty soon the old cat came over and rubbed noses with the dog like they were old friends. Grandfather said, "I believe that dog has been around here before, I have never seen a cat take to a stray dog that it didn't know."

Mom came out and told me if I had anything to do I better get busy as we had to leave in about an hour. I walked out to the barn and cleaned the stall and in front of the barn. I gave Horse some grain and brushed him lightly. Sandy came out and talked to me while I brushed him.

She said, "Johnny I am really proud of the way you handled things out there".

I was embarrassed and I told her I had been just as scared as she was. I was worried that the horse was going to get hurt, and expected the lion to run away, and when he didn't it was too late. I had to keep pressing him or he would have attacked us. I 'm just thankful that the dog showed up like he did, but it's a wonder the lion didn't kill him. He is a pretty big dog and I think he gave that lion all it could handle.

Mom called, and we had to go. We didn't talk much on the ride back to town, I asked Mom to not tell Sandy's mom that what happened was really a danger to us, or she wouldn't let Sandy come out to ride anymore. She agreed to go easy on the details, and let Sandy tell her what she wanted: she would just tell her a lion attacked one of the horses while we were off hunting arrowheads.

When we got to Sandy's house Mom went in with her and talked to her mother. She told her that the kids had had some excitement; that a mountain lion jumped on one of the horses while they were grazing down by the lake, and that a dog and I had chased it off. That is what happened in a round about way. Sandy's mom didn't seem to be upset by it she just asked Sandy if she got to see the lion.

After we got home, Bob had left me a note to get a ladder and clean the rain gutters on the house. I got the ladder but when I tried to climb it I couldn't stand the pain in my foot. I pulled off my shoe and sock and my whole foot was blue and black and really swollen bad. I hobbled into the house and told Mom that Jake had stepped on my foot a couple of times during all the excitement and I thought it was broken.

She took one look at my foot, and scolded me for not speaking up sooner. She made me get in the car and she drove me to the hospital. They took an x-ray of it. I had two broken bones in the top of my foot and a dislocated toe. The doctor pulled my toe out and twisted it. I almost came off the table it hurt so badly, and then he x-rayed it again. My foot was swollen too much to put a cast on it, so he wrapped and taped it, and put an inflatable cast on it. I would have to wait for the swelling to go down before he could put a regular cast on it. They gave me a pair of crutches and told me not to be putting any weight on it, and to keep it elevated until the swelling went down some.

CHAPTER X

Moms made me sit in a chair with my foot up, and read a couple of books she had checked out of the library for me. One was a story about a boy and a wild dog. I really liked reading it. The other book was about a pirate ship. I had never seen the ocean, even though we only lived about two hundred miles from it. So I didn't relate much to the story. Bob got home and took one look at me and said, "Boy some people will do anything to get out of a little work". Then he laughed and asked me what happened. I told him the whole story. He said, "John it's a good thing you didn't try and run from that lion or he would have killed you." This made me nervous now, when I thought about how dangerous it really was. I guess I didn't have time to get scared.

I had been laid up for about three days when Sandy and Jill came over. I got the crutches and hobbled out to the front porch and sat down on the porch swing. They wanted to know what happened to me. All I said was that a horse stepped on my foot. Then I had to explain all about it. I just told Sandy that Jake stepped on me that day out by the lake and it broke two bones in my foot. She didn't say much because Jill was there, but I could see in her expression she had a million and one questions. So we just sat there and talked until they had to leave. I hobbled back in the house on one crutch, Mom told me we had to go back to the doctor tomorrow and I would probably get a walking cast put on it. I didn't know what a walking cast was, but if it would let me walk without the crutches I was for it.

I got the walking cast and it made things a lot better; so much better, that Bob told me I could still mow the yard. I would have it on for about six weeks. There goes my summer. I probably won't get to go riding with Sandy anymore anyway, if her father finds out about everything that happened. I don't think he likes me too much anyway. He never talks to me, even when I try and talk to him about things.

Mom took me to the library and I checked out three more books. I got one about North American wildlife. I wanted to read up on mountain lions to see how dangerous they really were. I got one on the Modoc war; it is about the Modoc Indian war with the U.S. Army and was fought here in Oregon. The last book was about Indian treaties, how they were made and broken. I wanted to learn all I could about the treatment of my people. I plan on going to law school after I get out of college. There aren't many Indian lawyers, and I am sure the tribes need attorneys from their own race.

I sat around and read for a couple of weeks, keeping my leg up. I wanted the bones to mend straight and strong. I was a good runner and wanted to stay that way. Summer was going by quickly, and I went out to Grandfathers and took care of Horse every Saturday. I didn't ride much; just around the pasture and over to the agency store. The big dog was still hanging around, he would eat when Grandfather fed him, but I was the only person he would come up too. I could pet him but he would always move off, if someone else came close to him. Grandfather fixed a place for him to sleep in the stall close to Horse, as they seemed to like each other and Grandfather would see them playing out in the pasture at times. I never got to stay over there much, and there wasn't anything I could do in town. I hadn't seen Sandy for over a month, I guess they went on vacation someplace.

I tried to ride my bicycle but the cast wouldn't stay on the pedal, so I quit trying. I did hobble down to the park a couple of times and watched Larry and some of the other guys play basketball. My skin was starting to itch real bad under the cast. I was due to get it off in a couple more days, and I could hardly wait.

Mom took me in to get the cast off and the skin on my leg was all shriveled and funny looking, but my foot felt good when I walked on it. The doctor told me not to be running, or jumping around on it for a couple more weeks. I talked Mom into letting me go back out to Grandfathers; I wanted to ride Horse, now that the cast was off.

Grandfather was happy to see me and I was glad to get back out there. I cleaned Horse's stall and all around the barn, wheeling some of the manure out to grandfather's garden. I finally got to go riding. I put just a bridle on Horse, as I didn't need the saddle pad and it made him sweat under it. Horse and I took off across the desert with big dog leading the way. It seemed like he and Horse were racing, I just hung on and let them run. We went all the way to the river; I rode Horse out into the water and jumped off and splashed water on him. Dog didn't like having water splashed on him. He would jump in and swim but didn't like water in his face.

I caught Dog on the bank, and we wrestled around for a long time, he was really quick, and bit me kind of hard a couple of times. He would stand real still, and then jump on me hard enough to almost knock me down. I caught Horse and rode out into the high desert. Dog would take off chasing jackrabbits and Horse would follow him. I had a hard time staying on a couple of times when Horse turned real quick and I wasn't expecting it.

On the way home the dog jumped a big coyote and took after him. Horse was running and jumping sagebrush on one side and the dog was dashing through the brush on the other. That old coyote was going as fast as he could run, jumping and dodging brush trying to watch the dog and horse both at the same time. He made a quick turn and Horse almost run over the big dog, and we lost sight of the coyote so we went on home. It had been a good chase for a while. I put Horse in the stall gave him some grain and brushed him. Then I put out fresh water for the dog, and filled Horses trough, went in and talked to Grandmother she gave me a big piece of pie. It had been a good day.

Summer went by quickly. I went out to the reservation most every weekend and took care of Horse, and some times I didn't even ride him. I hadn't seen Sandy since I broke my foot. School was due to start in a week, so I had to go shopping with Mom for school clothes and supplies. We would be the big kids in school this year and next year I would go to the junior high or middle school as they now call it. I took all my books back to the library and went over some of my old school books especially the math book. I wanted to be ready.

School started and I had a very big disappointment; Sandy wasn't there! Jill said that she had moved away with her mother: that her folks had separated, and her mom moved back over to the coast. And to make matters worse, Charles, one of the kids I had the fight with was in my class, and just as mouthy as ever. He called me more names than Larry ever thought of.

I spent most of my time trying to avoid him; every word out of his mouth was cussing the damn Indians. I knew I was going to have to fight him again, or I would never get him off my back. Big Larry said he would take care of him if I wanted him to. I told him thanks, but I would try and fight my own battles.

I was eating lunch alone one day on the playground when Charles came over with a group of other boys and started in on me. I saw Larry walk up, so I knew if I needed help that he would keep the sides even. Charles asked me what I was eating. I didn't say anything so then he said, "What have you got in the sack Indian? Dog Meat?" Then he grabbed my lunch sack and looked in it; all I had left was an apple. He grabbed the apple and took a big bite, but before he could swallow or spit it out I hit him straight in the mouth, and pieces of apple flew everywhere. I grabbed him around the neck and punched him in the face several more times.

He was crying and trying to get away, and another boy tried to grab me, but big Larry took him out of the scene rather quickly. I just kept hitting Charles, and kicking him. I was really angry and wanted to hurt him. I didn't want anyone to think they could mess with me when this was over. Charles fell to the ground and I jumped on him and pounded him until Larry pulled me off.

I turned to the rest of the boys and told them that now is the time to take care of this Indian, or keep your thoughts to yourself. If anyone ever calls me a name again, he better be ready to fight. I was shaking and almost sick to my stomach, but I was going to set some people straight right now. One of the teachers came over, a Mr. Stewig; he took me off to the principals' office.

The principal asked me what I had to say for myself. I told him I was tired of being called, Indian lips, a blanket ass Indian, Tonto, and, a red nigger. That Charles had been picking at me ever since school started; that I was eating my lunch by myself, when he came over and took my lunch sack and started eating my apple. I tried to avoid Charles as much as I could, but he wanted a fight and he got one. The principal said that he was going to call my parents. I told him to do that, and to be sure and call Bob, my stepfather. Then I asked why Charles wasn't in the office with me. He said he is with the school nurse, and that he would be talking to him as soon as he could. I had to sit in a room by the principals' office until after Bob and the principal got through talking.

I had to go home with Bob, and he scolded me all the way home. I was still pretty mad and I asked him how much I had to take. He told me it wasn't about take this time, but about how much I gave. He said, "You beat that kid up pretty bad."

I said, "It would have been worse if Larry hadn't pulled me off him. I wanted this to be the last fight I ever had." Then I told Bob about the name calling, and other things they had done to me. That I wasn't going to stand and take it anymore if I had to fight someone every day. The day I took my quest to be a man, I made up my mind to never run from trouble again. I will do everything to avoid it, but if anyone touches me, or takes something from me, I will stand my ground and fight. I am "Two Bears" a member of the warrior society. I will not turn my back and run."

Bob just shook his head and told me that I was taking this warrior bit a little too far. I knew that as soon as Mom got home I was going to get another lecture and I was still mad. I took my books into my room and tried to study but I was too angry to read. I just sat there and went over everything in my mind. I didn't understand why someone didn't like me just because I was an Indian. I was smart, I made good grades, I kept myself clean, I didn't pick on other kids, and I tried to be nice and polite to everyone. I didn't look for trouble, but from now on I was going to face it, every time it came to me. And I knew it was coming, as soon as Mom got home.

Bob was waiting when Mom came in; they went into the kitchen and talked for a while. I didn't like causing situations like this. Why couldn't people just leave me alone? Mom called Grandfather and talked to him for over an hour. Then she called me into the kitchen and told me that she was taking me out to see my grandfather tomorrow. I was really ashamed now; I sure didn't want Grandfather mad at me.

I lay awake, most of the night worrying about facing Grandfather, what would I tell him? Morning came and Mom kept me out of school; drove me over to the reservation, and just dropped me off at my grandparent's house, she didn't even go inside. I sure hated to go in: Grandfather was sitting at the kitchen table drinking coffee. Grandmother got up and went into the bedroom leaving us alone. Grandfather asked "Are you having a bit of trouble at school Johnny?" I almost cried. I was so ashamed sitting here in front of him. I loved and respected him so much; I didn't want to cause any shame to him or myself. I told him the whole story just as it happened, and how I really wanted to hurt Charles.

He reached out and ran his hand through my hair and said, "Let's go have a little talk with Black Eagle, the tribal medicine man." We got in his truck and drove for over an hour out through the high desert, to a place I had never been before. It was along a river but I didn't believe it was the same river I played on.

Black Eagle walked out to meet us and shook my hand. He and Grandfather talked for a moment then he asked us inside. The inside of his house was decorated with animal skins, decorated bows and lances, even a buffalo skull with shiny black horns. His chairs were all covered with beautiful woven robes; there were many books on a shelf and bottles of stuff everywhere. There was a headdress of eagle feathers hanging on a stand, with long trains of eagle feathers stretched out clear to the floor. Black Eagle asked me about the fight I had in school. I told him the whole story, all about the name-calling and Charles taking my apple. He asked me, "Were you so hungry that you could not spare this boy your apple?" I explained that he had been calling me names, again.

He asked? "Are you so weak that you let the mere sound of a voice caused you to strike another? Johnny do you remember your quest when the cloud of snarling, barking, and growling animals came at you. You sat very still and watched them, and they caused you no harm. When the huge bear charged out of the cloud to engulf you with its fangs, you sat perfectly still and again no harm came to you. You sat while the elk nearly ran over you. And you never struck out until the huge dog licked you, and then you only struck him enough to drive him away".

"Did you not learn anything from this? By accepting things around you, and not reacting to them, no harm came to you. So is the way of life, let the voices bounce off of you, show them your inner self, show your strength, not by striking them but by being stronger than they are on the inside. If physically attacked, one has the right to protect himself, but do not let anger cause you to harm another person. Anger weakens you on the inside, and you cannot think clearly when angry. If you want to be a chief, 'Johnny Two Bears' you must learn and practice these things."

I bowed my head and apologized to Grandfather and Black Eagle. I told them these things I will remember and try to practice. I will always try and be mentally stronger than my enemies. I will not let anger cloud my thinking.

Black Eagle lit some sweet grass afire then blew out the flame letting the smoke drift over my body to purify me. He waved an eagle wing over me and fanned the smoke toward me. I felt clean and strong inside. I no longer felt any shame. I was ready to face my enemies, and protect my friends with an inner peace that I never had felt before. I would think through my problems, and not let fear or anger make a decision for me.

I thanked Black Eagle, and he assured me that if I had any more troubles to come see him. Grandfather drove us to town and we had lunch at a burger joint. I was really hungry, all this thinking really made me work up an appetite.

Grandfather took me home; he told me he would clean out Horses' stall for me this time, and for me to practice what Black Eagle had told me, to think about my quest, and learn to be a man. If they were going to call me names to look at them, and ask why do they do these things? Is it to make themselves feel better? Most people do this to hide their own weakness, and problems.

Mom took me back to school the next day and went in and talked to the principal. I never had any more problems after that. I only saw Charles on the playground, and I tried to stay away from him. They must have put him in another class, and he never bothered me, and the school year went by fast. I studied hard and made good grades. I tried hard to keep my mind and body strong and clean. I was now thirteen and would go to junior high next year.

I knew that going to a new school would bring new challenges, but some of my friends would be there. Billy would be there and I knew big Larry would stand by me. I would meet whatever challenges life threw at me.

CHAPTER XI

I was happy that school was out for the summer; the sixth grade had been a bad year. After my fight with Charles everyone sort of stayed clear of me. I could tell a difference even in the teachers. They seemed to only talk to me when I asked a question, other than that they just looked at me, and then looked past me. Some of them acted as if they were afraid of me, I could see fear in their faces. I tried not to offend anyone, in my manner of speaking or by my actions.

I had to do a lot of work around the house for Bob, and then Mom took me out to the reservation. Grandfather was glad to see me. He had made a pet out of the stray dog. The cat and dog got along good they would curl up and sleep together there on the porch, sometimes they would bed down with Horse out in the barn. I spent two days cleaning up the pasture and the barn area, and then I painted the barn for Grandfather. He would sit on a log by the fence and talk to me while I painted. Dog would wander off out into the desert and be gone for a day or two then he would show up again. Grandfather said he hoped he wasn't mating with a coyote; we didn't need any half-dog coyotes around.

On the third day I was there I took Horse and rode to the river, this time I took my fishing pole and some worms I had dug out of the manure pile. They were the little red wigglers, I would put three at a time on my hook and cast it upstream and let it drift down by the big rocks. I caught several trout about a foot long, and I must have caught twenty suckers. I threw them back but I kept eight of the biggest trout. I cleaned them in the river and packed them in a sack I had with wet green grass. Horse didn't like the sack, now that I had smelly fish in it.

I let him smell of it and look inside then it was ok. I think he was just nosey.

Dog had taken off again and I couldn't see him anywhere, I called to him but he never came. I rode Horse back to the house, and took the fish in and gave them to Grandmother. I went back out and brushed Horse down good and fed him some grain. It was still early in the day so I took my bow and walked out into the high rocks back of grandfathers' house. I shot most of my arrows at the little gray digger squirrels that live in tunnels under the rocks. I lost a couple of arrows and broke the tips on two more. I saw three deer feeding down by a spring that seeped out of the hillside. I tried to put the creep on them but the wind kept swirling around and they would smell me.

I watched the deer go drink, and then one of them squatted and took a pee. I crept down to the wet spot and rubbed the urine and muddy dirt onto my legs, I even rubbed some onto my arms and chest. It smelled bad but I wanted to smell like a deer. I would only move toward the deer while they had their heads down feeding. It wasn't long until I was almost close enough to touch one of the yearlings. I drew an arrow from my belt, and nock-ed it to my bow, I pulled the bow to full draw and held on the deer's chest. I stood there ready to end this creature's life, but I slowly let the bow down as it wasn't deer season and we didn't need the food. I did practice creeping along with the deer and they never knew I was there. The old doe would look in my direction but as long as I didn't move she never saw me. I heard something behind me or I guess I sensed it, just as I turned a big coyote jumped and grabbed me by my arm, I dropped the bow and tried to pull free, he just kept shaking and biting my arm harder. Blood was running down my arm as the fangs begin to tear my skin. I was scared and was yelling and trying to get free. The more I pulled the deeper I got bit. Fear was controlling me; I kept screaming, striking and kicking at the coyote. Then I saw another bigger coyote coming toward me, he was coming through the sagebrush as fast as he could run. Suddenly I was knocked to the ground by a mass of fur, teeth, and snarling, biting coyotes. I lay there on my back hitting, kicking and screaming; all I could see was dust and coyotes. I tried to get away but they kept knocking me down.

I rolled free after I hit the ground, as the coyote had turned loose of my arm. All I could see was dust and gray fur, it was a mass of fighting, the two coyotes were fighting each other, as I turned to run I recognized the big dog; he had came to my rescue again, he kept mauling and chewing that old coyote until he looked dead. Dog kept biting at the coyote for a long time, he would grab it by the back and shake it, and bite its neck then he finally turned and growled at me. The coyote lay dead, anyway I think it was dead I wasn't about to touch it and Dog wouldn't let me get close. Blood was running down my torn arm and I was covered with mud, deer urine, blood and dirt. Soon Dog came up to me and licked my hand, he still had all his hackles up and he had a lot of blood on him. I started to run for grandfather's house with Dog by my side.

I hollered for Grandfather before I got to the house. Grandmother came out the back door; she threw both hands to her face and let out a loud scream. Grandfather came out the back door on a dead run, almost taking it with him. "God John what happened?" He asked!

I said, "A coyote attacked me"

Grandmother came out of the house with a pan of water and a cloth and began to wash me; I was still bleeding pretty badly. Grandfather grabbed a towel and wrapped it around my arm, saying we got to get him to the hospital. Grandmother still wanted to clean me up first. If I hadn't been so scared it would have been funny. My arm hurt so bad I could almost scream. The white towel was all ready soaked with blood as Grandfather put me in the truck. Grandmother jumped in on the other side still washing me with the cloth as we hurried to town in grandfather's pickup.

As we got close to the main road we saw a police car. Grandfather flashed his lights and waved at the patrolman. We must have been going eighty, the police car pulled up along side of us, and when he saw all the blood, his lights and sirens came on and it was a ride I won't forget. I never knew Grandfather could drive that fast. I was getting so scared my arm quit hurting. Grandmother was still trying to wash me, but the cloth she had been using was now so dirty, and bloody that it put more on than it took off.

We got to the emergency room with the siren still screaming as we pulled in. The doors of the hospital flew open; people in gowns came running out, they pulled me from the truck and placed me on a bed with wheels and rolled me into a room that had the brightest lights I had ever seen. Grandfather was trying to talk to the doctor and the policeman; and Grandmother was crying and yelling at everyone. I looked down at my bloody arm and I could see several long deep cuts torn in it above the elbow, and a couple of holes down by my wrist.

The nurse was washing my arm while another put pressure on it with a white cloth. The Doctor asked me how old I was and what had happened to me. I told him a coyote had attacked me. The next thing I knew was someone calling me John and asking me to wake up. My head was spinning and I was getting sick, but my mouth was so dry I couldn't even spit. I opened my eyes and Grandfather, Mom, Bob, and Grandmother were all standing there looking down at me. My arm hurt really bad. I looked at it and there was a white bandage wrapped around it as big as my leg.

I went back to sleep, then I felt a cool wet cloth being moved across my head, and face. I tried to suck some of the moisture from the cloth; my mouth was so dry I couldn't talk. I finally asked for some water, but was told we had to wait a little while or it would make me sick. I was sick all ready; I needed some water so I would have something to spit up.

I shut my eyes and Bob said, "John you need to wake up and stay awake for a little while, so don't go to sleep on us."

I was in a daze; I was so tired all I wanted to do was get a drink and go to sleep. My arm hurt every time I tried to move it. I tried to force my eyes open but they wouldn't stay open. I could hear voices but I couldn't make out what they were saying, someone kept washing my face with a cool wet cloth, and Bob kept telling me to stay awake. I woke up enough to see a bandage on my leg and I could feel something tight around my chest. I went to sleep again; I could see Dog fighting this coyote. He had it by the middle of the back slinging it back and forth then he slung it toward me. I jumped and nearly came out of bed.

Grandfather was standing there holding onto my hand, tears made dark streaks down his weathered face. He looked so old. I wanted to rise up and hug him but I went to sleep again. Then I was in the cave with the bees, and the human bones, the bees were stinging my arm and shoulder and the skull was trying to say something to me. I could hear it calling my name; I opened my eyes and Mom was standing there washing my face with a cloth, as tears ran down her cheeks.

Why was everyone crying, and where was I? I looked around and there were bottles with stuff in them and tube's running down to tape on my hands. The back of my hands felt like bees were stinging me under the tape. I wanted to pull the tape off, but I was too weak to move. I looked over at Grandmother and told her not to cry, she stood up and walked over to my bed and hugged me. I told Mom to give the washcloth to Grandmother, as she likes to wash me. Everyone laughed, and Bob said, "He is going to be all right"

I still wanted a glass of water, so the nurse gave me a little glass of crushed ice; I never knew ice could taste so good.

The doctor came in and asked how I felt. I told him I was thirsty and sleepy. He asked Bob if I had said anything else about the attack. Bob turned toward me and asked me about what had happened. If the coyote was acting strange before he attacked me.

I said "I never saw it until it had me by the arm" The doctor told Bob that they should see if they could find the spot where I was attacked, and to see if a sick or dead coyote was there. I told them that Dog had killed the coyote, and then I asked how badly Dog was hurt, for he was bleeding pretty badly when we came to the house. Grandfather assured me that Dog was ok, but that he would go look after him right now.

Sleep overcame me, and when I awoke the room was dark and quiet. Mom and Grandmother were sitting in chairs over by the wall. Grandmother was asleep and Mom was reading a book, over by a lamp that was so dim I almost couldn't see her. I called out to her and she got up and came over and held my hand. With her other hand she ran through my hair and asked me how I was doing.

I said, "I'm ok".

She asked, "If I knew why the coyote had attacked me?

I said, "I have a pretty good idea, that it thought I was a deer"

I told her all about rubbing the deer urine, and dirt all over me so I could get close to the deer. I said, "With all the dirt and smell on me, and I had been stooped over and crawling to get close to the deer I was stalking. I probably smelled like a deer and all that the coyote saw was me moving through the sagebrush. I never saw it until it grabbed me. I was sure glad that Dog showed up, I think that coyote would have tried to eat me."

Grandfather showed up when morning came, and Mom told him all about me smearing the dirt and deer urine on myself.

He said, "We found the dead coyote and took it to the health dept. They took the head so they could check it for rabies. We also took the dog to the vet. He has several pretty good bite marks and a couple of deep cuts on him. The vet wants to keep him for a few days until we see how the coyote checks out."

My grandfather came over by the bed, put his hand on my shoulder and said, "John I hope you learned something by this." I didn't know what he meant by that. I really hadn't done anything wrong as far as I could tell. My experiment worked as far as sneaking up on the deer undetected. I would wait and talk to Grandfather more about it after I got home. I had to stay in the hospital a couple more days, to see if I got infection in any of my wounds.

Billy and his mom came to see me. He had gotten a lot bigger and looked different to me. We talked about the coyote attack and about the middle school. Billy told me I could play tackle football now that I was in the middle school. He was going to be the eighth grade quarterback next year. I told him I didn't know much about football, and I was pretty small.

He said, "Yea but you will be the fastest man out there! When we get to high school, with me throwing, and you catching and running no one will ever beat us."

I was allowed to go home the next day, so they took me out to grandfather's house, as Mom had to work, and they didn't want me to stay home by myself. I could get around ok, but my arm and leg were still bandaged. I don't know when I got bitten on the leg or my side, all I can remember is the coyote biting my arm and slinging me around. I had two bite marks on my side and several large bruises. Maybe Dog bit me while he was fighting the coyote.

I walked out to the porch and sat with Grandfather while he smoked his pipe. I asked him what he meant by me learning from this.

He took his pipe from his mouth and said, "John when you change your smell to that of a prey animal, you put yourself in danger of being attacked by a predator. You no longer have the man smell, that animal's fear to protect you. So you must be ever alert to the fact that you might become preyed upon. I think that is why the coyote attacked you. He either saw you as a danger to himself or as an animal he could eat. You were so interested in sneaking up on the deer that you failed to be alert to the dangers that were present around you."

"You must remember that the lion is still out there, and I don't believe it will attack a man as long as it recognizes you as a man, but if it sees you as weak, or mistakes you for a prey animal, its instincts are to attack and kill. You are growing into a fine man John but you still have many things to learn, so that is why I said, I hoped you learned from this. What you did was not wrong, but you failed to take time and think about what could go wrong. All through your life you will want to try new things. But before you do, you must think them through, as to what can go wrong and who will be injured it they don't work out."

I sat there and thought about what Grandfather had said. I had never given any thought to anything but creeping up on the deer. If I had been looking out for myself as I was creeping along, I would have seen the coyote in time to protect myself.

I endangered the big dog as well as myself, by not thinking about what could go wrong. I had gotten us both injured. I felt dumb and ashamed. How could I ever become a leader of people if I couldn't even see danger coming? I got up and walked over and put my arm around Grandfather and told him I was sorry that I had put everyone through this. He told me I needed to apologize to Grandmother, Mom and Bob. I had scared everyone pretty bad.

He said, "Boy you were a sight to behold, coming across that field with all the mud, and blood on you. You looked like one of Custer's boys, at the Big Horn. I thought that horse had fallen with you again, and then I saw him standing in the pasture looking at you. And that big dog he was almost as bloody as you, only he hadn't been rolling in the mud. And John you stunk worse than an old rut buck. How you ever snuck up on a deer smelling like that beats me. I believe that old coyote thought you were dead, and bit you just to make sure he wasn't seeing a ghost. I am surprised that old dog didn't dig a hole out there somewhere and bury you in it."

He laughed. It was good to see Grandfather laugh. His black eyes would really sparkle. It made me feel good to be close to him. I wanted for him to always be happy. I know he misses my father, even though he never speaks of him. Sometimes I think his memory is just too painful for him to bear. I gave Grandfather a hug and said, "Thanks, for what I didn't know." It seemed the right thing to say at the time.

I went into the house and put my arms around Grandmother, and told her I was sorry that I had scared everyone so bad. Then I kissed her on the forehead and said, "Thanks for the washcloth bath too".

She laughed and swatted me and said, "Now I suppose you want some pie for all your troubles?"

She got up and cut me and Grandfather a big piece of apple pie. I took it out on the porch and gave Grandfather his piece, and sat there and ate beside him.

He said, "John it seems like I eat a lot more pie when you are here. Maybe I will just have to keep you here all the time. Only I would get skinny patching up all your bruises. If it isn't Horse falling with you or some kid giving you a black eye, you go and pick a fight with a coyote." He put his arm around me and said, "But as long as you can keep Grandmother baking these apple pies I will keep you around."

It felt good being close to Grandfather.

CHAPTER XII

Grandfather took me back to the doctor after a week, and he took the stitches out of my cuts. I had a couple of pretty mean looking gashes down my upper arm, and one on my leg. That coyote must have sharpened his teeth before he grabbed me. It was fun sneaking up on the deer, but I will be more alert next time. I didn't like the fear of being attacked, and my arm still hurt, especially when I moved and tried to lift something, I had a lot of bruises on me, I must have really tumbled around out there, more than I thought I did.

The doctor said that I would be ok but to quit wrestling those coyotes for a day or two. Grandfather asked me how I felt and I told him that a hamburger would make me feel a lot better. We went over to a restaurant, where Grandfather likes to go. There are a lot of his old friends that hang out there. I still had a bandage on my arm, but you could see the cut on my leg and I had a couple of bite marks on my ribs. Everyone wanted to know what happened, so I had to tell the whole story again and show them all my bite marks. I left out the part of putting the deer urine all over me. They didn't need to know every thing. I really like being around these old friends of Grandfathers. I like hearing their stories and watching their expressions. Most of them have led a hard life and it shows in the lines of their faces. But most all of them have a gleam or sparkle in their eyes, especially when telling a tall tale, or when they are picking on one another. They wouldn't trade the life they have lived for all the money in the country.

I wish I could record all their stories, especially the true ones. Some of these men had fathers that were with Captain Jack in the lava bed strongholds during the Modoc war. They tell a lot different story than most of the books that have been written about it. I guess everyone has a different story, or how they remember it anyway.

When we got home I took Horse out for a ride. I could get around pretty good even though I did have the bandage still on my arm. Dog looked well he had a couple of pretty good cuts from the coyote but they were healing and didn't seem to bother him any. Early summer is a beautiful time on the Oregon high desert. Everything is blooming and still green, and there must be a hundred different kinds of butterflies and other flying insects, and there are a lot of newborn fawns and other animals to watch. I even saw a coyote, and my heart jumped with fear when I first saw it. I realize the coyote attacked me out of hunger, or just to see what I was, I am not sure. I rode Horse over toward the coyote and it ran before we could even get close. This made me feel better.

I sure wish Sandy hadn't moved. It was a lot of fun riding with her. I never knew I cared so much about her until she was gone. Now I spend a lot of time thinking about her. I remember how good her hair smelled and she always wore a good smelling perfume or something like that; what ever it is that girls put on. I think when I get back to town I will go see if Jill has heard from her. I didn't see Jill at the junior high so she must still be in the last school, she may have been a grade behind Sandy and me.

As I rode along the river, Dog went for a swim. I rode Horse out into the water and he stood there and splashed with his front foot. I would have liked to go for a swim but I couldn't get my bandage wet. After Horse drank, I rode him downriver to where the cougar got after us. I was ever alert for sign of the big cat, but never saw anything. I rode back upon the rocky hill where I had found the old cave, and checked on the bees. They were still going and coming so guess they hadn't been disturbed by anything. It would be like some old bear to try and dig in there to get all their honey. So I got off Horse and piled more rocks against the opening. Horse still remembered the bees, and as a fly buzzed his ear he took off running, with me running after him. Sometimes I really get angry with that dumb, 'chicken horse'. Dog took after him and got in front, and started barking, and turned him back toward me.

I finally caught him, and once I was on his back, I made him run as hard as he could. He likes to run and was jumping bushes and really going. I was hoping no badger had a hole out here or we were in trouble. He finally slowed down and we just walked along looking at all the country. I had never been in this part of the reservation, but I pretty much knew where I was. I rode up on top of a hill and dismounted and tied Horse to a bush, which he didn't like, but I didn't want to have to walk from here and I just didn't trust him today. Another fly might buzz his ear.

As I sat looking out over vast miles of open sagebrush and tumbleweeds, I wondered why the government, wanted to take this land from my people! There was so much of it, and you could only farm what you could get water too. There is a lot of wild game out here, and about every kind of bird that I knew about. There are a lot of sage hens, and quail. I liked to listen to them calling to each other. I would imitate their whistle and call back to them. It would have been a perfect day if Sandy had been here with me. I wished I could quit thinking about her all the time. Was I in love?

Horse must have read my mind, as he looked up and blew through his lips like he was giving me the ole' raspberry. I laughed at him, got up untied him, mounted and headed for grandfathers house. I was riding Horse real slow past an old shack that had long been abandoned, and as we came around the corner of the house, Horse scared a skunk that let us have it with both barrels. Dumb Horse jumped sideways so quick I fell off almost on top of that skunk, and got sprayed again. Dog came around the corner and grabbed the skunk causing it to spray some more. Horse took off for home leaving me, and Dog there gagging and spitting and trying to see. Dog was whining and rolling and pawing at his face and I was doing about the same. I sure wished I had some water. This was the smelliest skunk I had ever came close too. My eyes burned like they were on fire, and I was trying to throw up and could hardly breathe, the old skunk just sauntered off like he owned the world and as far as I was concerned, he did! I sure wasn't going to try and take it away from him.

When I came in sight of grandfather's house, I could see him leading Horse toward the corral, he was holding him at arms length and holding his nose as he walked. Dog went running up to him and he chased him away. What was he going to do when I got there?

Grandfather saw me coming, or he probably smelled me. He said, "Don't tell me you got sprayed too." I tried to explain that Horse dumped me right on top of the skunk.

He said, "I thought you were a better rider than that" Then he laughed. I felt better; he made me take all my clothes off and brought a bucket of hot water from the house with some bleach in it, and gave me a bar of soap and a brush and said, "Start scrubbing Chief. You will never get in Grandmothers house smelling like that." I washed and scrubbed myself; I took the bandage from my arm, the cuts and bite marks were pink and still swollen a little, but they looked like they were healing ok. I just left the bandage off. The odor of the skunk was wearing off or else I was getting use to it. I could no longer smell it except on my clothes. I put them in the bucket to soak and slipped into the bathroom and got in the shower.

Grandmother brought me some clean clothes. She was laughing at me and telling me about Grandfather getting sprayed by a skunk one time in the chicken house. I felt clean when I got out of the shower, but I could still smell some of the skunk on me. I didn't brush or wash Horse; I just let him and Dog enjoy their smell together. I went out on the porch to sit with Grandfather and he was holding his nose when I came out. He thought that was real funny, even the old gray cat wouldn't stay in my lap, he jumped up on me, took one whiff jumped down, and stood there looking at me, like he was trying to decide if it was really me or not. I walked out back and rinsed out my clothes and hung them on some bushes to air out. My hands smelt skunky again so I had to go scrub them some more. I see now why they make perfume out of that stuff, the smell lasts for days.

I walked out back to see how Horse was doing. He came over to the fence and nickered at me, like trying to say, "Hey stinky where are my oats?" Dog was nowhere to be found. He probably went back out into the desert to find something smellier to roll in. I didn't grain Horse I just left him in the pasture to wear off the smell. I would try and brush him tomorrow if he smelled better. I know one thing I will be more careful about riding around old buildings. Skunks don't like to be surprised.

When I went to bed I could still smell skunk on my hands, so I kept them away from my face. I got up early and fed and watered Horse cleaned his stall and brushed him good. He didn't smell too bad. I took some grain out and fed grandfathers chickens; the old red rooster was ready for a fight so I kicked him a few times when he tried to flog me. I don't think chickens have any intelligence at all; the more I fought with that old rooster the more he wanted to fight. I finally kicked him good and chased him into the chicken coop. But I sure didn't turn my back on him as I left. Then I forgot to get the eggs and had to go back in there again. This time I watched him closely; he cackled at me but didn't jump on me, as I never turned my back to him.

Grandmother fixed me eggs, sausage and pancakes for breakfast. Grandfather came into the kitchen still holding his nose. We both laughed and he asked me if I was going to go skunk chasing again today.

I said, "I don't think so, and I doubt if Horse wants to go either." I heard something outside and looked out. Dog was standing by the back door, and when I opened it the smell almost rocked the house. He must have been back over there killing skunks all night, or else he rolled in it. I finished breakfast caught Horse, and rode to the river with the dog, I rode Horse out into the water and Dog decided to join us, which I was hoping for. He swam a little bit then ran up the bank and rolled in the grass, he smelled a little better then but I still didn't want to pet him.

Mom came to pick me up, and of course had to hear all about the skunk episode. She scolded me and said, "John I think you could get into some kind of mischief sitting by yourself in a closed box!" Grandfather and I just laughed at her.

Grandfather had to go over to the coast for a day and asked me to go with him. I had never seen the ocean so I jumped at the chance to go. I promised Mom that I wouldn't get into any trouble, and that I would mind Grandfather.

We left early the next day; it took almost four hours to drive to Coos Bay, the town the man lived in that Grandfather needed to see. It was a nice town and a big river by it with several ships tied up to posts with wooden walkways out to them. Grandfather took me down to the ocean; it looked up hill, and like it would spill over onto us at any minute. I even got to walk along the shore, and run from the waves, while my grandfather and his friend sat on some logs and laughed at me. I sure wish Horse and Dog were here with me. They would have loved to run and play along the straight smooth sandy beach. There were sea gulls everywhere; Dog would have run hisself to death trying to catch them. Huge waves of water would wash over the rocks and come toward me so fast sometimes I couldn't out run them. I got wet and the sand stuck to my bare feet and felt funny.

The air tasted salty on my lips and the ocean water was real salty. I picked up little flat shells that Grandfather said were a clamshell. There were animals swimming in the ocean and climbing onto the rocks; they had no legs, just flippers! I guess they were seals, or sea lions, I couldn't tell which. I had seen pictures of them. There were little spider looking bugs that ran sideways along the beach, that were called sand crabs. They had a large pincher on them like a crawfish. The air was cool and the wind blew all the time we were there. I loved the ocean and the beach. I wanted to stay here and never leave. But my grandfather called to me and we had to head home.

He asked if I was hungry; which he already knew the answer. We went into Mc Donald's for a hamburger. I couldn't believe it, for there sat Sandy and her mom. She didn't see me at first. When she did she jumped up and ran over and hugged me; this kind of embarrassed me in front of Grandfather. She called her mom over and they sat at our table, and talked to us while we ate. Sandy wanted to know all about Horse and the dog. Grandfather had to tell them about the skunk, and me. I didn't like that, but everyone got a laugh out of it. Sandy's mom told us that they might be moving back over to where we lived, as she and Sandy's father had worked out their problems; this really made my day. I walked outside with Sandy as the grownups talked, while they were paying the bill. I told her I had missed her and she said, that she thought of me every day. This made me feel good. We then said goodbye to them and headed for home.

On the way home I must have talked to Grandfather a mile a minute. I asked him a million questions about the ocean and the things I had seen. This was a whole new world to me. I had seen pictures of the ocean on television, but for some reason the real thing is a lot different than they show on television or the movies. Getting to see Sandy again was a real bonus, and the thought of her moving back to town made me feel good all over. I finally slept part of the way home; this truly had been a great day.

Summer passed by quickly, and I managed to stay out of trouble most of the time. Horse, Dog and I just traveled all over the reservation, swimming, fishing and enjoying the life we had. I was looking forward to going to the new middle school. I wanted to play football and be in the same school with Billy, as we didn't get to see much of each other all summer.

The thought of seeing Sandy and of being in class with her really gave me something to look forward to. I worked hard for Grandfather. I painted Horse's barn and cleaned the stall and put all of the manure pile on his garden for him. We bought a truckload of hay from a rancher in Klamath Falls and hauled it to the barn and stacked it inside so it would be easy to reach. I had to build a panel so I could keep Horse from getting into it and wasting it. I started running every evening to get into shape, so that football practice wouldn't be so hard on me. I practiced running and dodging sage brush and jumping over tumble weeds, all the time watching out for badger holes and skunks, I sure didn't want to land on another one of them.

Dog ran with me; sometimes he would bump me and almost make me fall, so I watched out for that, and used it to my advantage. I would dodge him every time he came close. I got good at dodging him and jumping over him at times. I had started to grow a little now and weighed about a hundred and twenty pounds. My arm still bothered me where the coyote had bitten me. I had injured the shoulder muscles trying to pull free of it, and they hadn't healed all the way like they should. I was afraid to tell anyone. Afraid they wouldn't let me play football. I had to have a physical so thought I would ask my doctor about it.

Mom came over and got me during the middle of the week. I had a lot of stuff to do around the house for Bob, and Mom wanted me to hit the books a little before going to the middle school. Bob had an old set of weights out in the garage so I dug them out and started lifting. My left arm was a lot weaker than my right so I worked it hard, and my shoulder really hurt after I quit. I was scheduled for a physical the following week. I didn't work that arm as much after the first time. I wanted to ask the doctor about it first. Mom took me into the clinic for my physical on Monday. The doctor said I was in excellent shape, and I asked him about my arm.

He had me lift up against his arm, and said that I had probably damaged a tendon during the wrestling match with the coyote. He gave me a list of exercises to do twice a day and told me to lift a little weight also, but do it a lot of times not to try and lift too much at first. That repetition was better than lifting heavy weights.

Mom got me signed up for school, and football practice started that day so I was a day late in going out. One of the coaches came in, gave me all my gear, and showed me how to wear it. I didn't know if I could run with all that stuff on me or not. I went out and ran with all the other kids; about all we did was run and do pushups and stuff like that. One of the coaches kept watching me, so I asked Billy who he was, as he looked real familiar to me. Billy told me that was Charles' father; one of the kids I had gotten in a fight with at the park.

CHAPTER XIII

Charles was a year older than me, as was Billy and they were both bigger, but I was a lot faster than Charles, and I was as fast as Billy. We had to run a mile in nine minutes, which was easy for me; Billy came in just a couple of steps behind me. Poor old Charles or Chucky as his father called him was really struggling. He was in poor condition, I actually felt sorry for him. I don't know if he made it under nine or not but he managed to run the mile. We would run wind sprints, where you have to run hard for twenty yards, stop than run another twenty. I was always way ahead of everyone but Billy, and he was about twenty yards behind me. All the coaches except Chuck's dad had good things to say to me.

I could tell that Chuck's father didn't like me very much, and he was going to coach the seventh grade team. Lucky for me that we only had three seventh grade games, and the rest were seventh and eight grades combined. Practice was a lot of fun, my muscles was sore from some of the stretching exercises, but I liked the contact. I was quick enough that most of the kids couldn't hit me a straight shot. Big Larry did catch me not looking once, and really knocked me for a loop. I learned to keep a good look out for everyone after that.

Chucks father was called Coach Charlie, and he didn't seem to pay much attention to anyone but Chuck. I worked hard, even diving for the ball when it was thrown to far out for me to catch, once in awhile I would catch one while I was diving for it. The other coaches would praise me for it, Coach Charlie would just yell at Billy for throwing it too far. But if one of the other quarterbacks threw it wrong he wouldn't say a thing. It didn't take Billy or me long to realize that he just didn't like Indians. We heard him complaining to the other coaches, about how those damn Indians are fast, but they can't be depended on when you need them most.

Our first game was a seventh and eight-grade combination with a western Oregon school. My grandparents, Mom and Bob were all there, and as were expected Billy and I neither one got to start. But dear old Chucky was out there on every play. The other team scored first, and coach put Chuck back to return the kickoff. Why he didn't put Billy or me there everyone wondered, as we were the fastest players he had. The ball came right to Chuck, hit him in the shoulder pads and bounced back down field. One of the other players picked it up and ran right past Chucky, who made a halfhearted grab at him as he went by. We were now down two touchdowns and the first quarter wasn't half over.

We were behind twenty-one to nothing at half time; the coaches yelled and insulted us in the locker room, like it was our entire fault. Heck I hadn't even gotten in the game. Coach Chandler told Billy he would start at quarterback the second half. This made me feel a little better, until Coach Charlie piped up, and said, "The first screw up you make, your butt will be back on the bench."

Billy did a good job; even threw a pass down field to one of the backs and he ran it to the four yard line. On the next play Chuck took it to the one, the next play Billy had trouble with the hand off to Chuck so he ran it in for the touchdown. Coach Charlie came unglued, he was screaming at Billy saying 'that's not what I called', like he wasn't happy with the touchdown! Billy tried to explain, but was told to sit his butt down on the bench.

Billy just sat there, shaking his head. I walked over and told him things were ok, he said, that all the coach cared about was for Chuck to score. I sure wanted to play but the game kept dragging on, and everyone except me had been in the game. There was time for about two more plays, when Coach Chandler sent me in as a defensive back. I wasn't sure about what to do, but I knew if someone came out for a pass I was to knock it down, or at least make a tackle on the receiver.

Their quarterback called the signal and one of their ends came running right at me, he turned toward the sideline just in front of me. I could see the quarterbacks eyes looking straight at him, and he threw the ball just as I started toward him; the ball was under thrown and I managed to pick it out of the air. I turned on all my speed and streaked down the sideline. I could hear the people yelling, as I looked up one of the other players was in front of me coming straight at me with his head down, I stepped sideways and went past him; he never touched me. I ran clear into the end zone. I had scored a touchdown in my first game. I ran for the bench still carrying the ball; Coach Charlie screamed at me to give the ball to the officials; coach Chandler picked me clear off the ground and said, "Good job, Chief!"

Billy was grinning from ear to ear, and even Chuck slapped me on the back. Big Larry picked me up and almost broke my ribs, with a big hug. The gun sounded and everyone was still cheering like we had won, and we should have. Billy came up and said, "We may not have got to play much Chief, but we showed those pale faces how to put points on the board." Everyone on the team was excited as we went into the locker room. Coach Chandler told us we had done a good job; all coach Charlie said was, "what a good tackle that Chucky had made."

I looked at Billy and winked, then we both laughed, and Coach Charlie looked at us like he was going to throw us out of the dressing room. He asked what we found that was so funny so Billy just said, "Chief had his jockstrap on backwards or he would have run faster." Everyone but Coach Charlie laughed. Bob came into the locker room about that time and told me what a good run I had made, so Coach Charlie let up and walked off.

Grandfather took us all out for burgers, and everyone in the burger joint was congratulating me on my touchdown. Billy and his folks came in; we played a video game while the grownups talked about the game. I went home with my grandparents, as I had to clean Horses stall the next day.

At grandfather's house, I took Dog for a run out into the high desert. We must have ran for two miles before I sat down and rested, it was a beautiful morning and I had to get back and clean the stall. I loved the clean fresh air of the high desert; everything seemed so crisp and clean in the early morning. Songbirds were chirping everywhere and there were insects of every kind flying around, the air seemed to be full of bugs and birds. I thought about the people in the big cities that never get to see anything like this. I knew I could never live in the city; the small town was bad enough. Out here you were a part of God's creation not something made by man.

After I had rested, Dog and I took off running again toward grandfathers. I pretended I was carrying the football. I was dodging bushes, and jumping over weeds, I was really making the yards until that stupid big dog ran between my legs. I hit the ground harder than anyone had ever tackled me in practice. Dog let out a yelp, stopped and looked at me, like why did I do that? And why was I lying there on the ground? Then the dumb mutt came up and licked me in the face. I got up and swore at him and took off again, only this time I watched out for that four-legged tackler. I ran hard all the way back to grandfather's house. I was really pushing myself; I wanted to be a good football player. I was fast and had some good moves but I needed to learn more about the game.

I got busy cleaning the barn and stall; it was noon before I knew it. Grandmother called me for lunch and I was starved. I ate the two sandwiches she made me and drank two glasses of milk, and then she pulled a pie out of the oven. I didn't know if I had room for it but I took a piece of it anyway. After lunch I took Horse out for a run, he was really feeling frisky and wanted to jump and buck, so I held on tight with my legs and rode like the wind; we really traveled down the road and out into the desert. I let him run as long as he would, and it took some of the spark out of him. I rode clear over to the agency store. I wanted a cold drink but didn't have any money so I asked the store man if I could pay for it later. He laughed and said he would put it on grandfather's bill. I didn't like doing that, but I told him ok and I told Grandfather about it when I got back. He said that he would find some more work for me to do to pay for it. Then he laughed.

Sunday I went to church in town with my grandparents and they took me out to eat after church they dropped me off at home. I got on my bicycle and rode over to Jill's house and asked her if she had heard from Sandy? She hadn't come to school yet, and I wanted to see her in the worst way, but Jill hadn't heard a word from her. So I rode back home and done some more homework so I would be ready for school tomorrow.

Now I liked going to school, and I looked forward to football practice. Billy and I had decided if we tried to make Chuck look good maybe his father would notice it, and reward us for it. So we took extra care in blocking for him, and Billy always tried to throw the ball soft enough so that he could catch it. It was funny to see how excited coach Charlie got each time Chucky done something good. Chuck was a big kid and sort of awkward, but he had a lot of desire to play. He never bothered me much now so I tried to be nice to him and to get along with everyone. I never put him down like some of the kids did. Most of us tried to help him in practice and explain things that he didn't understand. One thing for sure, he was getting the opportunity to learn, he was involved in every phase of practice. He never stood on the sideline like I had to; he was always on the field.

I only got to alternate once in awhile in the drills, and every time I got a chance I ran as fast as I could, and tackled as hard as I could. I could catch the ball good too and really worked hard in practice. I always tried to lead the drills, and gave it my all. We had a seventh grade game in Medford on Friday, and as usual I stood on the sideline for most of the game, then our number two back got injured during the third period so I got to go in. Chuck was the number three back, or fullback, and coach called his number most of the time. We ran a sweep right, which was away from my side of the field; the quarterback kept the ball and then pitched to Chuck as he was hit. Chuck made the turn, and I was fast enough to get past him and take out the linebacker. Chuck was in the clear; as I looked at the sideline after I made the block, Coach Charlie was all ready in the end zone. He had run all the way along the sideline with Chuck. I thought it was funny and was laughing as I came off the field. Coach Charlie actually slapped me on top of the helmet and said, "Great block Chief, you made that score happen."

After the kick off, he put me in as a defensive back and I managed to make a couple of tackles and knocked down a pass. We had failed to make the extra point, so I knew if they scored we would probably lose this one too. I cheated up close to the linebacker and watched the quarterback; he didn't show any sign of passing. I read the run to my side, and came up quickly to hit the flankerback, just as they tossed the ball to him; he fumbled and big Larry was on it. We now had the ball with only a few seconds left in the game. Everyone one was jumping and yelling; we finally settled down and just knelt on the ball twice and the game was over.

The locker room was a madhouse. We had won our first game, and old Chucky had the only touchdown. Coach Charlie was ecstatic; he even had a good word for the Indian. He told me I had played the best game of anyone and that I was going to start in the next game. Maybe Billy's and my theory was working! It was a fun time, I really felt like part of the team. We stopped at the burger place in White City and ate; everyone was talking a mile a minute. I just sat back and listened to everyone; it was just a loud roar. We really had fun on the ride home.

Going out for the team had been good for me; a lot of the kids that used to call me names now talked and played with me. I felt like I was finally being accepted. Only thing was I got to thinking too much about football and I almost failed one of my tests. Mom told me that if this happened again I would have to quit and work on my studies. I didn't want this to happen, so I tried to really pay attention in class and not get to thinking about playing football. I went over my homework several times each evening, just to make sure I was right.

School had been going now three weeks and Sandy hadn't shown up. I was really disappointed, as I had looked forward to going riding, and being in school with her. I asked my mom to call her mom and see if she had moved back yet. She told me to call her father and ask him. I picked up the phone several times but chickened out each time.

I would go over and have Jill call, that way it wouldn't look so bad.

I rode my bike over to Jill's house and we talked for a while, then I ask her if she had heard from Sandy. She said that she had tried to call her number and the phone had been disconnected. My heart sank a little deeper; what if I never got to see her again? I really liked her, she was so much fun to talk with, and I always enjoyed our rides that we took together, especially when we were both on the same horse. I liked the warmness of her arms being around me especially when she held on tight. And the smell of the perfume that she wore. I talked to Jill a little longer than rode home.

Mom took me out to Grandfathers so that I could take care of Horse, and I asked to spend the night, so she talked to Grandmother a while and left me there. I cleaned the stall and everything in front of the barn then I grained Horse and brushed him while he ate. Grandfather came out and asked if I wanted to ride with Mr. Fox and him over by the lake to where I had seen the lion. It sounded like fun so I agreed to go with them. Soon Foxy showed up with Jake and another horse he was riding. Grandfather got on Jake and we rode slowly out toward the lake. It took about an hour to get there; I showed them the muddy flat and cattails where the lion had attacked Jake.

We rode around in the high rocks for a long time looking for the lion. Dog finally showed up and tagged along with us; suddenly he bristled up and growled and took off running up a steep pile of rocks. We dismounted and climbed up to where an old lava flow had made a cave. Dog was standing in front of the opening growling and barking. It was dark in the cave and we couldn't see much. Grandfather tied Jake to some brush took his rifle out of the scabbard, and walked into the mouth of the lava cave. The further in the cave Grandfather went the more dog barked, and tried to stay in front of him. Mr. Fox took his rifle and walked up over the cave to see if there was another opening. Grandfather came back out and asked if I would ride back to the house and get a couple of flashlights. I got on Horse and slowly walked him down to flat ground and when I kicked him in the ribs with my heels, he sensed the urgency of our trip, and took out as hard as he could run. We were jumping sagebrush and tumbleweeds; the clumps of desert grass were just a blur as we raced past them. Horse ran hard all the way back to the house. I jumped off, and Grandmother came out all excited, and I told her we needed two flashlights, as we thought the lion was in one of the lava caves.

I got two flashlights and got back on Horse; he was still lathered up from the hard run so I just let him go at a walk for a while then picked up the pace. I never made him run much on the way back. When I got back to the cave Mr. Fox and Grandfather were sitting in front of it smoking and talking. Dog was lying in front of the cave just inside enough to get out of the sun. I wanted to go in with them but Grandfather told me that Horse needed cooled out, and for me to take all three horses down to the lake and let them drink and to walk Horse slowly, then get some handfuls of grass, and wash the lather off him, and to rub him down good or he would get stiff on me. I didn't want to go just then but I knew not to disobey Grandfather.

I untied Mr. Fox's horse, got on Jake and rode to the lake with Horse walking along behind me. I got off and led the two horses out into the water and let them drink then I tied them to some brush and pulled up a big handful of grass and waded back out to where Horse was still drinking. I dipped the grass in the water and rubbed Horse down good; he splashed water on me with his front foot. I worked as fast as I could, maybe I would get back in time to see them shoot the lion. I untied Jake and the other horse, jumped on Horse and rode back up toward the rocks. I hadn't heard any shooting, but when I got back, Grandfather and Mr. Fox were sitting there smoking, and a big dead lion lay in the shade with Dog standing by sniffing of it. Grandfather showed me the worn out teeth and a crippled foot the lion had. He said that was probably why it had tried to kill the horse, as it was in real poor shape and was probably starving to death. We drug the lion down to a grove of juniper trees and skinned it there. Mr. Fox said it was too old and poor to use any of it for food. I never knew that people ate mountain lions! But I guess they are all white meat like a rabbit, and are really tender. Grandfather took the skin and the skull to give to the fish and wildlife people for their studies. The horses did not like being around the dead lion and Jake wouldn't let you get close to him with the skin. So I carried it on Horse. He rolled his eyes and looked back at me holding the skin, and decided if I was brave enough to hold it he was brave enough to carry both of us.

When we got home Grandmother took a few pictures of me holding up the lion skin. I wanted one of the claws so Grandfather cut one off for me. I scraped it clean and he drilled a hole in it; put it on a piece of string and made a necklace out of it. Now I could tell all the kids about the lion hunt. I just wished Sandy were there to hear all about it.

CHAPTER XIV

I helped Grandfather scrape and salt down the lion skin for the Fish and Game people. Grandfather said we really didn't have to do this, but it was much nicer for the people that had to handle it. I just think Grandfather still likes doing things in the old way. When the mills were running we would have big picnics and barbecues, everyone would dress in the old traditional way, and there would be hours of games, dancing and singing. The elders would tell stories of long ago, many of them had been told back several generations, now due to the environmentalist, and there do-good ways most of this has been lost to the world forever.

Stories have been written about a lot of it, but most of them are bias to the writer's feelings. I have heard and read so many stories about Captain Jack and the Modoc wars, that I have no idea what the truth is, and few of the elders do either. Even if their grandfathers fought with Captain Jack, most of the truth has been lost through people changing how they tell the story. I still wish these big get-togethers would happen again. It just seems like everyone is too busy trying to find a job and make a living. Neighbors have forgotten how to have fun in the old ways, when everyone depended on each other for food and safety.

I liked to hear the story of the great encampment, when everyone went over the mountain, to the great Rogue and Umpqua rivers, where they spent all summer catching and drying salmon. There were many battles fought over certain fishing holes, and shallows along the river. In the fall as the tribes moved back to the high desert, they would hunt the elk, as they traveled along the high Cascades. Many uses were made from the elk including the antlers, for making packing frames, tools, and weapons; the teeth were used as jewelry, and the skin was used to cover lodges and for clothing. Many of our elders can't write the words and the young people who can, aren't interested enough to record their stories and the history behind them.

I loved to hear of the brave deeds that were performed by great warriors, both in and out of battle. We were once a great and proud people. Then the white man came, he wanted to farm the land and this polluted the water, soon the salmon were few and the sights of the great encampments were plowed under and put into crops, and we were no longer welcome along the great river. We could no longer camp and fish on lands that had been free since the beginning. The Indian could not understand how someone could own a part of the earth. How could you own something that you could not pick up and carry with you? How can you say this piece of earth is mine, and you cannot walk upon it? Most of this land was taken from the tribes without a bill of sale. Even the treaties marked out boundaries, giving back to the Indian his own land. Now these lands are part of our National forest. Does the nation hold a bill of sale showing these lands were purchased from the Indian? These things I intend to find out, and have ruled upon by the great courts of our land. I will study the white mans laws; I will also study the Indian laws and the treaties that were signed. Some day I will lead my people "I will be their Chief."

I sat there on Grandfathers' porch holding the old gray cat, dreaming of the great deeds that I would do. I would try and write down some of the stories that the old ones tell.

Grandmother called me to come eat, and this jarred me out of my dreams, and deep thoughts, especially knowing that she had baked another pie for dinner. After dinner I went out and made sure that Horse and Dog had feed and fresh water. I cleaned up the stall, and around the front of the barn.

I went to church with my grandparents and then they took me

home. I had a lot of homework to do, so I wanted to be ready for school the next day. Football practice was a lot more fun this week I got to participate more; I worked extra hard giving it all I had. I tried to always be around Chuck in case I could block or do something for him. I wanted the coach to notice everything I did, I wanted to start in the next game, but it was a 7th and 8th grade game so there would be more big kids.

It was a home game, and we were playing a team from over on the coast. I never even thought about Sandy, until I checked out their cheerleaders and one of the girls looked just like her. I kept staring over at them, and the coach yelled at me and told me to pay attention to the game. As usual most of the plays were called for Chuck to run up the middle. Finally Coach Chandler sent me in the game and told me to run a deep flare pattern. Billy and I had been staying late and practicing a pass play where we marked a spot on the field and I would cut either right or left, which ever we had called. Billy would throw the ball just as I made my cut. I took the play in and it was called twenty-four flanker, flare right. Those meant for me and the four backs to flanker each side of the field and go straight toward the defensive back and cut right.

I forgot the snap count so watched the ball, just as it moved I tore out as fast as I could run; I ran straight at the defensive back and cut right flaring over the middle. The ball was already there as I made my cut, it lit in my hands and I was in the end zone. Billy had made a perfect throw! We went for two points with a thirty-five dive. Chuck was the three back and went through the five hole. This was to the right of the center. I led the blocking and took on the nose tackle. I didn't move him much but got in his way enough that Chuck went through. I made a point to end up on the other side of the field and as I ran back to the bench I took a long trip by their sideline. It was Sandy! I wanted to stop everything and talk to her. I hollered 'Hi' and ran on over to our bench, as I looked back she was waving to me.

Coach Charlie saw all of this, and jumped all over me, asking me if I wanted to go over and be on their cheering section. This made me mad and embarrassed me; most of the players laughed at me, and I got teased for it. They didn't know how much I wanted to be over there. I didn't get to play defense, but when we held them I went back to return the punt. The ball came to me and I went straight up field until I came to the first tackler, then I cut hard toward the sideline and used all my speed. I had everyone beat if I could make the cut. I turned up field and really turned it on, I thought I had scored but the official called me for stepping out of bounds. It must have been when I looked up to see where Sandy was. I came out of the game a little disappointed but Coach Chandler called Twenty-one sweep and sent me in to run it. That was a run around the left side of the field with the other three backs leading the blocking.

The ball was hiked to me; I had to delay a count to give the other back time to get in front of me. I followed my blocker around the corner, this time I didn't look for Sandy, I just ran hard and when I saw a hole through the center of the field, I made a cut to go down the center and there was their middle line backer; but big Larry came bursting around me and it sounded like a train wreck, the line backer flew backwards with big Larry pushing him. I was in the clear and we had six more points. We ran the extra point with the same play we had on the other one. Only this time Billy faked the ball to Chuck and ran it in behind him. We were ahead fourteen to nothing at half time. The rest of the game dragged on, with Chucky getting to carry the ball most of the time. I was anxious for the game to end so I could go over and talk to Sandy.

The other team scored and made a two-point conversion, it was late in the game so I knew I wouldn't get to play anymore. I just waited for the sound of the gun and after we congratulated each other and shook hands with the other players I kept watching Sandy, as she walked off the field. The dang coach wanted to talk, and so did I, but not to him, or any of the other players.

Sandy was almost on the bus before I caught up with her. I ran up and said, "Hi, good to see you again."

She said, "You looked good out there today".

I smiled and said, "Well I had someone to show off for."

We stood and talked until she had to get on the bus, then I stood beside it and talked to her through the window. She didn't know when, or even if, she was going to move back over here.

I was late getting back to the locker room and Coach Charlie chewed me out, saying that I would rather talk to the girls than play football. If that was the case he would see if he could get me on as one of the cheerleaders. This really made me angry, and I wanted to say something, but I just smiled and got undressed and took a shower. Coach Chandler came in and talked to Billy, and me about the pass play, he wanted us to keep practicing it every chance we got. All I could think about was Sandy so I didn't hear half of what was said. It sure made me feel good to get to talk to her again, and I really hoped that she would get to move back over here.

I went home with Grandfather after the game, so I had a lot of work to do, taking care of Horse, and doing a few other chores for Grandfather. It was getting cold now and the desert was covered with a white frost every morning. Horse liked to get out and run in this weather so I rode him a lot. The sun would come out, and melt the frost that it hit, leaving a silvery shadow around each bush and rock. I would ride over to the river but it was now too cold to go into the water, so I would just let Horse go out far enough to drink. Even Dog wouldn't take his dip in the water anymore.

One day I rode Horse down south, on the reservation to where I had never been before, to some lava caves that Grandfather had told me about, they were large enough that I could walk inside them. I didn't have a flashlight so could only go so far; but the sides of the caves were as smooth as glass, and looked like melted chocolate had been poured down them. Some of the caves went down pretty steep and then they were frozen over with ice. It was cool down there and I wondered how thick the ice was. Dog and I spent all day exploring around these caves; some of them were caved in at places to where you could climb out, leaving a large opening there in the ground.

I had put hobbles on Horse with my belt so that he wouldn't wander off to far, so I had to keep checking on him. I don't think he liked being hobbled, as he would look at me for a long time, each time I came out to check on him. I don't think many people had been to the lava caves for there were still old stone tools, and bowls stashed behind some of the rocks. Some of the walls had paintings and drawings on them, showing a great sheep or goat with huge curved horns. I guess they were old drawings made of the desert sheep. The next time Billy or Sandy came over to ride, I wanted to bring a flashlight and go through some of the long dark caves. It was getting late in the day, and the sky had turned a dark gray and it started snowing before I got started for home. The snow made it hard to see very far, so I wasn't sure which way to go as I could no longer see the distant hills, so I just let Horse pick his way, hoping he was smart enough to get us home. It got darker and started snowing harder. I was getting cold. Dog had long since left for home I guess, as I hadn't seen him since the snow first started.

The wind was now blowing the snow and making it much colder. It was hard to keep going against the snow at times and Horse would turn and walk with his side to the wind, and then he would turn and walk straight into it, going from side to side. I was getting scared, as it was now almost too dark to see more than a few yards. I could hear Dog barking and Horse headed straight toward the sound. We came out right by the barn, and I was one happy Indian. I gave Horse a little extra grain, and put fresh bedding down in his stall. I shut him in the barn to keep him warm and made a place for Dog to get inside out of the weather. Grandfather came out to check on me, while I was brushing Horse down. He said, "John, I thought 'Ole' Two Bears' had gotten himself lost out there."

It was snowing hard and a couple of inches now covered the ground, it was good to be inside and Grandmother had a pot of chili made and a peach pie. I was in heaven! I ate until I couldn't eat anymore. Grandfather and I watched television until we both fell asleep. Grandmother came in and turned off the television and told us to go to bed. Sunday morning there was about eight inches of snow on the ground and it was still snowing lightly. Grandfather decided it was too cold and slick to drive to town for church so we watched a pro football game on television. It was one of the first football games I had ever watched, that grown men played, they sure were big and tackled a lot harder than we did!

After the game I walked out to the barn and let Horse out. He ran, jumped and bucked all over the place with Dog barking and chasing him. I laughed at them, and threw snowballs at both of them. I wanted to go riding but had to clean the stall. After I had everything clean and fresh straw put down for bedding I grained Horse, then went into the house, and asked Grandfather for permission to go riding. He told me to stay away from the river now that it was icy, with snow along the bank that Horse would slip and fall in with me.

I put a saddle pad on Horse, and rode out into a new world with Dog running along barking at us. There were animal tracks everywhere. I had never seen so many rabbit tracks; they were everywhere, like a million rabbits had been running and playing. I just rode slow looking at the snow-covered beauty of the high desert. The sagebrush and juniper trees were mashed down with the weight of the snow, looking like little white buildings. Sage grouse were gathered under the junipers; I guess they were eating the berries that fell off. I saw several deer and watched two coyotes chasing a jackrabbit around through the snow-covered brush. They were having a hard time keeping up with the rabbit and soon lost him. Dog took out after the coyotes until they turned to fight him, then he came back to where Horse and I were waiting. I guess he didn't want to tangle with two coyotes at once, and I couldn't blame him. The coyote has very sharp teeth that are made for slashing and cutting, as I can show you by the long scars on my arm. They can cripple and kill a deer in a very short time. A fawn doesn't have a chance once a coyote sees it. They will kill them sometimes just for fun, not eating a bite of the meat. I have seen a pack of coyotes run a deer until it is exhausted then take their time killing it, only to just lap up the warm blood and not eat the meat. Maybe they come back and consume it later. The mountain lions and bobcats will rake leaves and sticks over their kills to hide them from other predators; only the smart little fox always finds it and helps itself to a free meal.

It had started snowing hard again and I was a long ways from Grandfathers', so I turned toward his house, and ran Horse for a long time. I let him run at an easy lope, until I was in sight of the barn.

I put Horse in the clean stall, brushed him down good, and fed him some more grain. Dog came in and lay down in the corner of the stall and was asleep before I could get Horse brushed. I shut them inside the barn to keep them warm. Dog could go through and out the back if he wanted out.

I hoped Grandmother had some more chili, and peach pie left for I was hungry. Grandmother must have read my mind for she had a bowl of hot chili and a cold glass of milk all ready for me when I came in. She made me go wash first, which I did in a hurry, wiping my dirty hands on a clean towel. I turned it over so the dirt couldn't be seen; maybe she would think Grandfather did it.

I ate two bowls of chili, drank the milk and had a piece of peach pie with another glass of milk. I was so full my stomach hurt. Grandfather was watching the news on television. I went in and sat down; the old gray cat came over, jumped in my lap and started purring as I petted him. Grandfather was almost asleep so I didn't bother talking to him, next thing I knew the television was off and Grandmother was telling me to go to bed. I lay there in bed worrying about getting back to town, and how I was going to get to school tomorrow.

I could hear the wind moan and howl as it blew around the corners of the house and barn. It made a sad scary sound as it screamed with each hard gust that blew. I was sure thankful that I had a nice warm bed in a warm house on a night like this. Soon the ringing of the phone awakened me; it was daylight now and I could hear Grandfather talking on the phone. I got dressed and looked outside the snow was over a foot deep and great mounds of it had blown up around the barn and the fence.

Mom was on the phone; she had called to tell us that school had been canceled and I could stay out there for a few days until the roads had been cleaned up and were safer. I wondered about football practice, but figured they would call me. We only had a couple of games left to play. I didn't think I would try and play basketball, as I wasn't a very good shot. I could handle the ball well, and was fast on the court, but I knew that Coach Charlie would be the coach, and that Chucky would get to play all the time.

I needed to study more and there were several books I wanted to read on the Indian wars. The more I read about some of the old days, the more interested I became in what had happened in the past. I wanted to go spend a day with Black Eagle, and talk with him. He was a wise old man, and had seen much, in the changes of our people, and the old ways.

I started writing down the things I wanted to ask him. I still had some things about my vision quest, that I needed answers to; especially about the great warrior who appeared before me, and the penetrating look of his eyes, as he saw clear through me. The decorations on his shield were like nothing I had ever seen before. Was he real or just a vision; and how could others before me see him if he was only a vision? Surely people don't have the same vision. Was all of this stuff in my mind all the time? And why did it take the stress of sitting out there until I was delirious, for me to see them?

I know that many of our tribal leaders had visions that helped them make the right decisions. They would spend many hours in a sweat lodge, to clean their mind and body. Sitting Bull had many visions of soldiers dieing long before the battle of the Little Big Horn. Were these really a vision or a message from a higher source? There isn't much written down about my people, most of it is kept in the minds of the elders, and passed down from one generation to another in stories. I want to capture all of these stories and save them forever. I must learn all there is to know about my people. If I want to lead them in the future I must learn about the past.

I will ask Grandfather first, and learn all about my own family, before I talk with Black Eagle and some of the other elders. First I must find out if it is ok to write all of this down. I also realize I have a lot to learn about myself, before I can learn about others.

Grandmother called to me and jarred me out of my deep thoughts, she had breakfast ready, and I was hungry. She had made hotcakes, eggs and some bacon. Grandmother was the best cook I ever knew; I hugged her and told her so. She ran her hands through my hair, and said, "Thanks, I suppose you expect another pie for that." We both laughed and sat down to breakfast.

After I had eaten about a dozen hot cakes I took a handful out to feed Dog and gave Horse one of them. He didn't like it at first but then he wanted them all. I told them they were better with syrup and butter, but I don't think they took time to listen to me. I chased Horse out into the cold snow, and watched him jump and buck as he ran around in it. Dog ran with him and liked to nip at his heels, so Horse would kick at him. Sometimes I think those two can communicate with each other. I cleaned the stall and filled all the water pans with clean water for all the animals. I cleaned the whole barn, fed the chickens, played kick the rooster when he tried to flog me again. There were only three eggs, guess the old hens were too cold to lay anymore.

I filled Grandmothers wood box from the wood in the shed, and then shoveled off all the sidewalks out to the garage, then cleaned most of the snow out from in front of the garage so Grandfather could get the truck out.

I could smell something good cooking in Grandmother's kitchen and believed she was baking another pie. I hoped she was anyway. Grandfather might be getting fat from all the pies but I wasn't. I could still stand to gain a few more pounds.

CHAPTER XV

It had finally quit snowing and was now colder than I could ever remember. I kept Horse in the stall and Dog stayed in there with him. My hands were freezing as I fed the chickens and looked for eggs, it was so cold the old rooster didn't even try and flog me. He just stood over in the corner with all his feathers ruffled up looking like he was froze to death. I only found one egg, the old hens must be frozen up also. All the water troughs were frozen, I took warm water from the house, poured it into a bucket for Horse to drink. I also took warm water to the chickens and made sure Dog had water.

The snow was frozen stiff and made a loud crunching sound as I walked on it. I couldn't stay outside very long, as my feet were getting numb and hurting real bad. I felt sorry for all the animals and birds that had to endure this bitter cold. I looked at Grandfathers' thermometer; it was twenty-two degrees below zero. I filled the wood box again, putting all the wood into it that it would hold; making several trips into the house to get warm. It was getting dark out now, and the cold continued to get worse. It hurt my lungs each time I took a deep breath, I walked out to the barn and made sure Horse had plenty of hay in his feeder and I put more straw down for him to lay on. Dog was all curled up in the straw not moving, he did look up and wiggle his tail a little as I walked in. Horse was standing there munching hay like he was in heaven. He didn't even look cold; his coat had grown out to where he had long hair on him and looked sort of shaggy. I shut the barn door and walked across the frozen crunchy snow to the house.

I thought about the stories that Dad used to tell about the winter he spent in Korea. It got so cold that the fighting all stopped and they would see the enemy soldiers out scrounging for wood just like they were. Sometimes they would even wave to each other. He said that they burned tires, motor oil and anything else they could find that would burn. Their clothing wasn't adequate for the cold conditions, and they were suffering badly. He said they would take the clothing off the dead, and wrap themselves in it. That when the wind would blow, if you spit, it would freeze, crackle and roll across the ice like marbles. I tried spitting and it wasn't cold enough to freeze.

He said they would get in groups of three's, and huddle together; they would change places so that every two hours you got to get in the middle and get the warmth from the two men on each side of you. This was how they slept; sometimes they only had one blanket for three men.

Dad said that he craved canned apricots, and one time Mom sent him three cans in a box of stuff. He ate the first two cans and carried the third can with him until it froze and burst; leaking out inside his pack. He poured the juice out when it melted, and ate the apricots dirt and all.

I walked into the house, it was nice and warm with a fire roaring in the wood stove. Grandmother had made me a cup of hot chocolate with some little white marshmallows in it. I sat at the table and drank the chocolate and nibbled on some sugar cookies that Grandmother had made. I really loved my grandmother; she was always doing things for me, like making cookies and pies. She always seemed to know what I wanted to eat, and when. I ask her how she knew these things; she told me that she had my dad to practice on, and that I was just like him. This made me feel good. I know they miss him a lot, and so do I.

I was tired so I went to bed early. I lay there under the warm blankets thinking of the soldiers in Korea, all huddled together in a foxhole while the cold wind blew snow over them. Some of them froze to death, while others lost their toes and fingers from the bitter cold. I hope I never have to go to a war, but if I do I will go and try to do my best.

When I awoke I could hear my grandparents talking out in the kitchen. I got dressed and went out to have some of grandmother's hot cakes. She had made some elderberry jelly, and I put it on my hot cakes. I ate more than I should have, but they were so good I just kept having one more until I was so full I felt I would burst. The sun was shining and the glare off the snow was blinding. I bundled up and took Dog and Horse a handful of pancakes. Horse wanted out of the barn until he smelled the hot cakes, then he turned and almost knocked me over trying to get them. I fed a couple to Dog before I gave one to Horse. By this time he was butting me with his head and pushing on me. I liked to tease him; he was such a pig when it came to eating.

The day was a lot warmer and the snow was starting to melt off the roofs where the sun hit it. I cleaned the stall while Dog and Horse ran around in the pasture. I tossed a block of hay out for Horse to eat on. I wasn't going to let him back in the barn as long as it was nice out. I didn't want to clean it again. I thought about riding him for a while, only the snow had made such large drifts in places that I didn't think I had better chance riding through it. I went back into the house and Grandfather said he would take me back to town if the roads cleared up. Bob was probably mad at me for not being home to shovel out the driveway and sidewalks at the house. The snow would be frozen too hard to shovel now. It had warmed up a lot and the melting snow was dripping off the roof and tree limbs. I called Mom and she said, if they had school she would call and let me know.

I really wanted to go home I was starting to get bored here all shut up inside the house. I liked to roam the reservation and watch all the wild animals and plants. I pulled on my coat and called Dog. We went for a walk. The snow was still stiff and crunchy; the mashed down tumbleweeds and sagebrush made it hard to walk and in places the snow was blown up into drifts ten feet tall. I would climb up on them and slide off like I was skiing. I must have walked two miles or more out into the desert. I never saw a deer track or animals of any kind. I did see a few magpies flying about. My feet were starting to get cold, so I headed back for Grandfathers house. By the time I got there my toes were numb and hurting like they were frozen. I went in and took my boots off and sat by the fire warming my feet. A couple of times I got my socks too hot so I jumped around and danced like a wild Indian. Grandmother sat and laughed at me. Even the old gray cat thought I had gone plumb goofy.

It had warmed up a little bit and a soft light rain started falling. Grandfather decided to take me home so I rushed out and made sure Horse and Dog were cared for and gathered up my books and clothes and we headed for town. The rain had started to turn to little ice pellets and they bounced off the hood of the truck: it was getting colder and the roads were turning to ice. We were about three miles past the agency store on a barren stretch of the reservation road, when we met another car coming our way and it skidded over and collided with our pickup, knocking us off the road. I remember feeling the truck turn up on its side, and Grandfather yelling something as we rolled down into the ditch. It was a terrible noise of breaking glass and crunching metal then all was quiet. I lie there on my side with Grandfather on top of me, among all the twisted metal, tools and broken glass. I tried to move but the weight of my grandfather held me down. I looked up and blood was dripping from his face and one arm was twisted in a funny way under him. I called to him and he didn't move or answer. I became very scared and started to fight my way out from under him. The shards of glass were cutting my hands and legs, but I managed to crawl free.

I tried shaking Grandfather but he wasn't moving. I looked out and the other car was on its top and someone was lying halfway out the window. I managed to get out of the pickup through the broken windshield. I crawled over and tried to talk to the other people in the car that had hit us. No one was moving. There was a lady and two children lying all twisted up in a pile of broken glass and blood. I didn't know what to do.

All I could remember was Mom and Dad being in a bad wreck. I ran back to the truck and pulled on Grandfather's arm. He moaned but didn't wake up. I knew I must go for help. I couldn't remember if the agency store was open when we went by or not. It was now getting dark and no one had come along. I started to run toward the store, the icy road was so slippery that it made it hard to run; I got on the shoulder and ran until my lungs were bursting. I kept going my chest was burning like fire with each breath I took. The cuts on my arms and face were bleeding badly. I was cold but sweating, my legs felt numb but I kept on running. I was aware that I was crying and the tears mixed with my blood soon soaked my shirt. I couldn't let Grandfather die, he meant so much to me, there were many things I hadn't asked him, or things I hadn't learned from him. My shoulder was now hurting from where I hit the dash of the truck when we wrecked. My breathing was coming in long painful gasps, I was getting sick and dizzy but I ran on. I would run until I became unable too. It was a lot farther to the store than I had remembered. It was now almost too dark to see and the rain had turned to snow. I was now soaking wet with rain, tears, blood and snow.

All I could think of was Grandfather lying there maybe dying. I was in agony and I could hardly stay on my feet but yet I found the inner strength to continue. Soon my stride became a rhythm with my heartbeat. I was sucking wind with great painful gasps, I could no longer feel my legs, and I fell going face down on the road. I felt the rocks and ice cutting into my face and hands as I slid along the frozen ground. I lie there crying and gasping with long sucking breaths. Suddenly a figure shown in front of me, it was the Great Warrior that

I had seen in my vision. He stood before me with his brightly decorated shield and sharp lance sparkling in his hand. He said, "Two Bears you must get up and continue this journey as other peoples lives depend on you."

With a renewed strength I arose and continued running, with the Great Warrior leading me, taking giant strides beside me. It was as if my feet no longer touched the ground, I couldn't feel my legs and I tried to heave as I ran, waves of sickness engulfed me but yet the great one would not let me stop. He urged me on, and I could feel the cold wet rain and snow pelting my face and I was aware of a deep burning in my chest and shoulder.

I wanted to stop and just catch my breath, only the warrior beside me kept me going. I could see a distant light through the darkness; it was so far I didn't think I could reach it. With great sucking breaths I increased my steps and speed. I had to save Grandfather. I was 'Two Bears' a member of the warrior society. I would never quit in battle nor would I quit now. With a renewed strength I ran on, then I was alone again; the Great Warrior was gone. Had he ever been there or was I hallucinating.

The light was getting closer I could still feel the warm blood from my cuts flowing down my chest against my cold skin. I tried to wipe the blood and water from my face, but my hands felt torn and frozen. I prayed to the Great Father of the universe to give me strength and for my Grandfather to live. I was still running but I could no longer feel anything. I could hear my breathing coming in long raspy gasps. Then at last the lights were in front of me. I burst through the door and said, "Wreck! Bad wreck up the road!" I didn't even know if anyone was there, all I remember is hearing the crashing sound as my cut broken body hit the floor.

I was aware of strong hands lifting me up and a voice saying: "How did he get here?" Again I tried to tell them of the wreck and about

Grandfather, and the other people. I tried to get up to go with them and show them the way. I was in a car being driven very fast. I wanted to tell them to slow down. Someone was standing over me looking down at me, only I couldn't see in the dark. I became aware of much pain in my hand and shoulder and my arm was tied down to where I couldn't move it. I tried to get up only strong arms held me down and someone was talking to me. Telling me I was going to be ok, I hollered, "Grandfather! What about Grandfather?"

The next thing I knew was I was lying in a bed with white sheets all over me and curtains pulled around my bed. Mom and Bob were sitting in chairs by the bed. I jumped and tried to get up; my arm was in a cast, and two of my fingers had metal things bent over them and were taped together. Mom asked me how I felt. I asked about Grandfather and she said, "He is going to be fine." I lay there for a long time thanking God, for looking out for us. Then I asked about the other people and was told that they were going to be all right also. That thanks to me for going for help everyone was found in time.

Bob told me that I had run over three and a half miles on ice and in below freezing temperature to get help. I wanted to tell him about the Great Warrior but I didn't. I would wait and talk to Black Eagle about it. I still wonder if all this happened; it was like a dream, only my broken arm and fingers wasn't a dream, and my face was cut and bruised all over. I had a deep cut on my leg and it was black and blue. The wreck didn't seem that bad, it all felt like slow motion. I do remember a lot of loud crashing noise and the breaking of glass and then everything was quiet

I was able to get out of bed with Bob's help, and to walk down to Grandfather's room. He was sitting up in bed. He had a bandage around his head and his eyes were black and swollen and he had a cast on his leg. He asked me if I knew what happened. I told him that the other car slid on the ice and hit us head on, and turned us over. He couldn't remember ever seeing another car. He had come to in the wreck, and found the other people and helped them; he had forgotten that I was even with him. I guess we were all pretty lucky as the car and pickup were really damaged badly.

We stayed in Grandfather's room until the nurse made us leave. I was allowed to go home the next day. I was worried about Horse and who would feed him. Bob drove out and checked on everything and talked with Grandmother. She told him that Mr. Fox had volunteered to come take care of Horse until Grandfather and I were well enough to do it. They let Grandfather go home the next day. He was bruised up pretty bad and his leg was fractured below the knee. My arm really hurt, but I didn't say anything; I just took the pain. I wanted to go back to school but Mom made me wait until Friday and then she drove me over. I had to explain to everyone about the accident; the football coach Mr. Chandler wasn't too pleased as we still had two games to play. It didn't seem to bother Coach Charlie. Coach Chandler told me I could wear my jersey and stand on the sideline with the other players. It was a home game that night and we managed to win by two points. Chucky got his touchdown and Billy threw for one and ran a sweep for another. We made all the extra points while the other team failed on two of theirs, other than that it was a pretty close game. I wanted to play in the worst way but with an arm in a cast I guess that would have been a bit much. We all went out for pizza after the game and I had to tell about the wreck a dozen different times.

Saturday morning we went over to Grandfathers. Bob drove me by where we had the wreck than showed me how far I had run. I couldn't believe I could have walked that far, let alone run that distance in the cold, and at night. The Great Spirits had truly helped me. I knew I must talk with Black Eagle. His medicine was strong, and my medicine had been strong on that night.

144

CHAPTER XVI

We stopped at the agency store, as I wanted to thank the people for helping me. When we came in the man and woman running the store got up, hugged me and made us sit down. Their names were Mr. and Mrs. Crawford, and they had only been running the store for about six months and didn't know me. I guess I scared them pretty bad when I came crashing through their door all wet, and muddy, and bleeding all over the place.

Mr. Crawford said that I looked like a truck had hit me, and when they tried to find the wreck, they looked all over the place, as no one could believe I had run that far. When the ambulance was coming for me they found the wreck and everyone in it. I guess Grandfather had climbed out onto the road and was waving them down. They had to send another ambulance out for me. Mrs. Crawford had washed my wounds and cleaned glass from some of them. I don't remember any of that but I thanked her for it and apologized for scaring them. She hugged me and said I was welcome anytime even if I didn't need help.

We went on over to Grandfathers. He was sitting watching television, with his foot up on a chair. He said, "This dang cast gets heavy!" I slipped out to the kitchen to see Grandmother, and maybe if she still had a piece of pie for me, which she did. I had a piece of pumpkin pie with whipped cream on it and a glass of milk. Then I took apiece in to Bob.

Mr. Fox came over to take care of Horse. I felt bad that someone else had to clean his stall, so I went out and tried to help him, but couldn't do much with one arm. I told Mr. Fox that as soon as I was able I would come over and work for him to pay him back, he laughed and said, "Just get well Johnny and we will work it out then." I liked Mr. Fox he was a hard worker and always tried to do things for other people.

I was able to brush Horse with my good arm so I did all the brushing and feeding. I even fed the chickens and took on that old rooster with only one arm; he seemed to know that I was injured so he was much braver; he tried to flog me as soon as I got inside the pen. I kicked him until the feathers flew, but a dumb rooster doesn't have any sense. He wouldn't quit until I hurt him then he just flew up on the roost and cackled at me while I gathered what few eggs there were.

I hate that dumb old bird, and I don't see why Grandfather keeps him. He couldn't whip a hawk if one came around. All he did was flog me, eat, and crow. I bet he would be too tough to even make chicken stew out of. Well he kept my fighting skills tuned up, so I guess as long as he lasted I would still have to go a round with him every day, until he learned to leave me alone.

I wanted to talk to Black Eagle so I had Grandfather call him. We talked on the phone and he asked me about things and I told him I had a lot of questions that needed answered and I didn't want to ask them over the phone; so I asked Bob if he would take me over there. I told Black Eagle that we would come over, but he said that he needed to see Grandfather, so he would come over here and then we could talk.

Bob filled the wood box for Grandmother and helped me clean all the water troughs for Dog, Horse, and the chickens. That dumb rooster didn't even make a move toward Bob all the time he was in the pen. But as soon as I came through the gate here he comes. I told Bob that I was going to kill that dumb bird one of these days. He laughed and said, "I can see why you would want to."

We had just finished cleaning and watering everything when Black Eagle showed up. He came in and talked with Grandfather for a while, then he said, "Chief lets go for a walk." We walked out into the high desert and upon a little rise behind grandfather's house. He sat down on a big rock and asked me what I wanted to talk about.

I told him all about the wreck and my run for help. I told him about the Great Warrior that came to help me when I fell and couldn't get up; how he encouraged me to keep running even after my legs were numb and my lungs were bursting for air. How he ran with me for a long time urging me on, talking to me to keep me running, how he told me that others were depending on me, to bring help for them.

I asked Black Eagle who this Great Warrior was. And why had he come to help me both during my quest and during my run for help? Black Eagle picked up a hand full of dirt and let it sift through his fingers as he looked toward the heavens. He sang an old Indian song as the dirt slowly fell from his hand. Then he looked at me and said, "Johnny Two Bears, what you saw as a Great Warrior was your inner self; you were able to call upon strength that you never knew you had. You were able to reach deep inside your own mind and body for strength to keep you going, in doing so you got a look at what you want to be. The Great Warrior is you!"

This I could not understand, and asked Black Eagle if he could explain it better for me.

I said, "This warrior didn't look like me. He carried a beautifully decorated shield and a lance that shined in the dark. He ran beside me taking great strides; how could this be me?"

Black Eagle said, "Did you not ask the Great Father for help? To give you strength and help you too help the others? And when you asked for his help, did you not expect to get help from him?"

I said, "I expected to be given the strength to make the run."

Black Eagle then asked me, "Why than do you question the way that the help came? Were you not praying during your vision quest for strength to get through all of the things that were happening to you?

When you need courage or strength and you are exhausted, you must reach deep within yourself for the powers that the Great Father has given you. In using all of your inner-self, you sometimes get a look at yourself that you have never seen. A strength that you didn't know you had and a power that only you can see and feel. The Great Warrior is in your blood, he was in your father's blood, and your grandfather's blood, and the fathers before them. They are the only ones who have also seen the Great Warrior.

He has never appeared to me, or anyone other than people of your bloodline. So Johnny, the Great Warrior is within you. This is about the only way I can explain it to you. He is a warrior of long ago, but his blood still flows in your veins. This is a very sacred thing, and must not be talked about freely to others that won't understand. You now know you have a power given to you from the ancient ones. It is in your blood to be strong and courageous. So Two Bears use this strength wisely, it will take you far."

"Johnny, when you are older you must come and study with me. There are many things you need to learn to help our people."

With this said he again picked up a handful of soil and turning toward the East, South, West, and North. He raised his hand toward the heavens and let the dirt slowly drift from his hand. He spoke words that I did not know, and then he walked from the hill as I followed. Somehow I felt like a different person. I thought of all the other warriors that I was kin too, that had come this way before me. Would I be able to follow in their footsteps?

It was late in the day as we returned to Grandfathers house, it didn't seem like we were gone that long, but Bob was anxious to leave so I told everyone good-bye and thanked Black Eagle. He grasps my arm up by the elbow and we shook hands or arms this way. It felt strange but closer than a regular handshake.

Bob asked me what we had talked about. I told him that it was all about Indian medicine, to make me stronger, so that I would heal faster. Bob asked me if I believed in all of that old Indian medicine man stuff. I tried to explain to him that most of it was still in use by doctors today; that they just fancied it up a little so white folks would pay more for it. Bob laughed and seemed to be satisfied by my explanation.

I went to bed shortly after we got home. I lie there in my bed staring into the darkness, trying to remember what the face of the Great Warrior looked like. I soon was asleep and dreamed of the Great One. I was running across the barren country in a fog, only my feet weren't touching the ground. I was moving through the air as if I was flying, the Great Warrior was beside me, smiling at me, only I couldn't see his face; it was like I was being blinded by the sun. Suddenly I was awake, the light was on in my room and Mom said, "Good morning sleeping boy it's a school day and you better get cracking, breakfast is ready. I went into the bathroom and washed up. I couldn't shower with the cast on my arm so I skipped that. I ate too fast and Mom told me to slow down; that I had plenty of time. Then Bob gave me a ride to school.

I had trouble carrying all of my books with only one arm, so I drug my book bag up the steps and to my locker. I took only the books I needed and went to my classroom and sat down. I hadn't studied like I should have so I tried to read up on things as best I could. Usually we didn't have a test on Mondays anyway. The day drug by slowly and finally the bell rang so I went down to the boy's locker room and then went out and watched football practice. We had only one game left, and it was a rival game with the county school. I sure wanted to be out there playing, but all I could do was stand and watch.

It was still cold out so I didn't watch practice very long. I took my books home and really studied. I didn't watch television all week. I knew if I didn't do well on Friday's tests that Mom wouldn't let me go to the game. The week dragged by and finally Friday got here and Bob drove me to the game. It was really cold, so I wore my heavy coat and stood with the players on the sideline. We managed to score first but they tied it up right away. They called a 'thirty-five dive', which was for Chucky to take the ball straight up the middle. We only needed two yards and they were looking for it. Billy gave the ball to Chucky then pulled it back and ran sixty yards down the side on a bootleg. Everyone was cheering except Coach Charlie. He was screaming at Billy before he ever got to the bench, he grabbed Billy by his facemask and pulled him to him and screamed "If *I tell you to give the ball to someone, then by god you better give it to him.*" He shoved Billy out on the field and said, "*Now run 'thirty- five dive' and give Chuck the ball.*"

I could see the look in Billy's eyes, Chucky was going to get the ball all right. Billy called the play and took the snap from the center; he turned and as Chucky came up to take the ball, Billy drove it into his stomach so hard it knocked him down, and he fumbled the ball. Everyone piled on the ball. Poor Chucky was lying there with the wind knocked out of him, crying and trying to breathe; all that air out there and he wasn't getting any of it!

Billy was in trouble and he knew it. I had to laugh to myself but I did feel sorry for Chuck. Coach Charlie grabbed Billy and asked him what in the hell was that?

Billy said, "Coach, I believe that was a fumble."

Coach Charlie was fumbling for words, when Coach Chandler sent Billy in to kick the ball. Chucky was standing on the side trying to puke, and breathe both at the same time. After the kickoff Billy came over to coach Charlie and said, "Coach I stumbled and almost fell; Chucky was closer than I expected him to be so the handoff was sort of hard." He looked at me, winked, and grabbed a drink of water.

Coach Charlie just stormed off to the end of the players and stood there glaring at Billy with his arms folded. We lost the game by one point, but in Billy's thoughts and mine, it was worth it. Billy said, "Man I feel sorry for you. You have to play for him again next year, but

Chucky won't be there, so maybe things will be different." I told Billy I had heard that coach Charlie was transferring to high school so he could help coach his son.

Billy said, "I am going to go to the county school if he does!" We both laughed and Billy headed for the locker room.

Bob drove us over to the pizza place where everyone goes after the game. We went in and ordered and sat in a corner booth. While we were waiting I decided to play a video game, and as I walked by a booth someone reached out and grabbed me and said, "Hi handsome, how you hurt yourself this time?" I was stunned, there sat Sandy! I hugged her with my good arm. I wanted to pick her up and run with her, to where I don't know. I just wanted to hold her, and talk to her, but there were too many people around, so I just stood there like a dumb Indian, and didn't say anything. I was in shock; all I could do was mutter words that I didn't even understand.

Finally her mom spoke up and asked if I had gotten hurt playing football?

I explained to them that my Grandfather and I had been in a wreck, when a car slid on the ice and hit us. I didn't go into any of the details even though I would have liked for Sandy to know about my brave, heroic run in the dark when I was scared half out of my wits. I took Sandy by the hand and walked her over to see Bob and my mom. After talking to my folks we went back over to where Sandy's mom sat and I noticed her father was sitting there. He said, "We were wondering why you weren't playing tonight. I guess we didn't notice you standing on the side with the players."

I told him that I sure wanted to play, but doubted if I would have been much help with a broken arm!

Sandy said that she was here registering for school, and that she would be coming back after Christmas break. Her father had gotten his old job back, and he and her mom were back together. I was so happy for her I could have squeezed her, and I really wanted to, but figured it was too embarrassing in front of everyone.

Billy and his folks came in and I called him over and told him to come see who was back. He looked at me and smiled, and then said 'Hi' to everyone. He was still pumped up about the game, even though we lost by a point. I told him we shouldn't be so rough on Chucky it wasn't his fault if his old man was a jerk. Billy said, "Yea, but I can't hand the ball off to the coach." We laughed, but I felt sorry for Chuck; he tried hard and did just what his dad told him to do. He was a big strong kid, but it just wasn't in him to be tough, which was a good thing. Probably the only mean thing he ever done in his life, was jump on me that day in the park after I kicked John's bike over. I think all of us were just a little bit jealous that he got to play so much.

Sandy asked if she could come over the next day, and I said, "Sure!" without even checking with my folks. This didn't go unnoticed by Bob, he said, "We're getting a bit anxious aren't we Chief," I blushed a little and said, "I guess so, but it's just been so long since I have seen her." Mom tried to cover for me, but it just made things worse, and everyone had a laugh at my expense; but if she comes over, it will all be worth it.

The pizza and soda were good and everyone talked a long time. No one seemed to notice the hard handoff to Chuck but Billy and me, so I guess that it was ok. I didn't want anyone thinking badly of Billy. We had a hard enough time with some of the kids without asking for trouble.

I went to bed shortly after we got home. I lay there awake thinking about Sandy and how good she looked, and how good she smelled. I had to figure out a way to get Mom to take us over to Grandfathers so that we could both go for a ride on Horse. I only had one arm but figured out we could ride double and be ok. I finally fell asleep. Mom woke me saying that she was going over to Grandfathers for a little while. I asked her to wait until Sandy came over so that we could go with her; that Sandy wanted to see Horse and the dog. It took some doing, but she finally agreed to wait.

Sandy came over about one. Mom called her folks, and made sure it was ok to take her with us. When we got to Grandfathers we went in and said, "Hello!" and then we were out the back door. I caught Horse and put the saddle pad on him and helped Sandy get on. Then I led him over to the water tank, climbed up on it, and jumped on behind her. Horse looked at me like I was on wrong, but we went on riding like this. We rode up into the hills behind grandfather's house, to a rocky bluff overlooking the reservation.

Here we got off and walked over to the rocks and sat down and talked for a long time. We had been gone about two hours and I knew Mom would want to leave so I took Sandy by the hand and helped her up. As she stood up she came close to me and kissed me. I was caught off guard and shocked so much I almost jumped back; she laughed and said, "What's the matter O Great Chief, hasn't anyone ever kissed you before?" I recovered fast and said, "No one as pretty as you," and I kissed her back. I helped her up on to Horse, but every time I would try to get on he would run sideways.

I tried leading him over to the rocks but he wouldn't stand still. I had Sandy get off and I got on, and then tried to pull her up onto Horse; he would run and jump around and we both fell off once and my arm really hurt. I think this stupid horse is jealous of Sandy. I took my shirt off and put it over his head so he couldn't see, then I led him over to the rocks and jumped on and Sandy got on behind me. He jumped around a little, until I kicked him in the ribs. He ran a ways then straightened up. It was a good ride back, with Sandy's arms around me, and the smell of her perfume. I was in heaven.

CHAPTER XVII

It really felt good being out here with Sandy. I don't know if I am in love or not, for I have never been in love before, all do know is I really like her, and like being with her. We rode slowly back to Grandfathers. Mom was waiting for us; she told me to hurry and get the chores done, as she was ready to go.

We put Horse away, and I managed to get him some grain and hay. Sandy brushed him down while I fed the dog and went out to feed the chickens. Of course that dang old rooster was ready to fight, and I was in a hurry so I tried to ignore him, but the minute my back was turned he was on me, flogging me and trying to rake me with his spurs. I swung the bucket I was carrying and hit him in the head. He started flopping all around and finally just lay still. I believe I have killed him, so I just kicked him over under the roost and hope Grandfather will think he died there. I peeked outside to see if anyone has seen me. I grab what eggs are there and put them in the bucket, while trying not to look at the still form of that old rooster. I am glad he is dead, only I hate to think of what Grandfather will think of me if he finds out.

No one talked much on the way home. Mom asked me if everything was all right. I asked her why she would ask that? as my heart jumped into my throat. Had she seen me kill that danged old rooster?

She said, "Well everyone is so quiet" I told her about us having such a hard time getting back on Horse; that with my bad arm I couldn't pull myself or Sandy back on him.

Mom said, "You should have thought about that before you got off. Why did you get off?" She asked. Sandy blushed and I fished for words finally I said "Oh! We just wanted to sit and talk, and I never thought about the getting back on; that was why we were so late getting back. We should have just walked, it would have been faster".

We dropped Sandy off at her house, and Mom ran in and talked to her mom. Sandy came out and said she would call me tomorrow. Mom had told me not to make any plans as I had a lot of studying to do. When we got home I did some chores that Bob wanted done and then I hit the books. I had a hard time studying as I kept thinking about Sandy and kissing her. Had I done the right thing? Maybe she would think I was getting too fresh and wouldn't want to go anywhere with me again.

I had to read the same stuff over several times as my mind kept wandering back to Sandy. Finally I just gave up and went to bed, only I couldn't sleep for thinking of the day and the fun we had. Then I got a sick feeling in my stomach as I thought about killing grandfather's rooster. He would surely know I killed it; Grandfather was a very wise man. I don't think he can be fooled, especially if he looks at that old bird. I never checked to see if there was any blood. I just hope and pray that he thinks that old rooster died in his sleep of old age. I should have told him what I done. I have never lied to my grandfather, and I wouldn't want him to think bad of me, but to tell you the truth I am glad that dang rooster is dead, I just wish I hadn't been the one to kill him.

I lay there in the dark thinking of things I could tell Grandfather, but finally decided I would just tell him that the old rooster flogged me and I hit him with the bucket. Then he will want to know why I didn't tell him so they could eat him. Now I was worried! Not only had I killed the rooster, but also I had wasted the meat. I didn't want to tell him I was afraid. How would it look for the great Two Bears, the one called Chief, to be afraid to admit that he accidentally killed a rooster? My beautiful thoughts of Sandy and me had been ruined by the dread, of a dead bird. How do I get myself into these messes? I work hard, study hard, and seem to always be in trouble. If it isn't a coyote biting me it's a rooster flogging me.

Sleep wouldn't come. I lay there in the dark, wanting to get up and call Grandfather to tell him about that dang rooster. Maybe I should go tell Mom or Bob. But they would think I was crazy waking them up this time of night. I tried to think of Sandy but my mind kept returning to that pile of red feathers that once was a proud, ornery rooster. I shut my eyes, and I can see him laying their one leg drawn up as if trying to kick at me, his long neck and head stretched out with that one eye looking at me.

I finally fell asleep and the dreams started coming. I was riding Horse and this rooster kept flying up into my face, and knocking me off of the horse. Just as I'd fall, I would jump and be wide-awake, my heart pounding in my chest. Every time I'd fall asleep I'd dream about that rooster, some of them didn't make any sense, and other dreams he is just chasing me, and every time I kick at him I wake up. The next thing I know Mom is hollering at me to get up. I dressed and went into the kitchen. She said, "What is ailing you? You look like you laid awake all night."

I said, "I did, I couldn't sleep for worrying about killing grandfathers old rooster."

"You didn't!" She said, "Why didn't you tell us?"

"I guess I was just too embarrassed, with Sandy being there an all. It was an accident; he was flogging me and I hit him with the bucket."

Mom said, "Well you better go in and call your Grandfather now, and explain what happened." I hated to do this but I called and asked him if he had been out to the chicken house. He said No, but wanted to know why? I told him I might of hurt that old rooster last night when he flogged me. Grandfather laughed and said, "Well that might explain things."

He said, that when Mr. Fox came over to water and feed them this morning, that the old fighting rooster just stood up on the roost with his head bent over sideways and looked at him. Grandfather told me not to worry about it, and laughed again. I was mad, that old rooster had won again. He wasn't even dead, and I had lain awake all night worrying about killing him! I was so angry that breakfast didn't even taste good.

I felt better after breakfast, so I hit the books and studied some more. I skipped church and read all my homework a couple of times. Sandy called and wanted to come over after church. Mom said that it would be ok, so I hurried around and got everything done that Bob had asked me to do. Monday was going to be my fourteenth birthday, and I asked Mom not to say anything, as I didn't want to go through all that birthday stuff at school.

Sandy showed up about one and we played a card game while I told her about my experience with grandfather's rooster, and all about how I thought I might have killed him, and how I lay awake all night worrying about it.

Sandy said, that she had to be home by two and asked me to walk home with her. Old dumb me jumped at the chance, and walked home with her, not thinking about anything but her. When we got to her house she asked me in and as we came through the door, a bunch of kids came out of the other rooms, and hollered "Surprise!" I guess I was! I couldn't figure out what was going on for a moment, then they all started hollering "Happy Birthday" I was a little bit embarrassed but excited too. I had never had a birthday party like this. Mom and Bob showed up, while were eating cake and ice cream. I had to make a wish, but didn't know what to wish for so, I just pretended to make one then I wouldn't tell them what it was. I thought about wishing that old rooster was really dead, but then I thought of all the sleep I had lost over him so decided I better not do that.

The birthday party was a lot of fun, all the girls lined up and gave me a little kiss on the cheek, while all the boys jeered at me, and made jokes to embarrass me. We played a lot of games, most of them I had no idea how to play, as they were all new to me. I realized that Indian kids play a lot of games that the white kids probably don't know either. I have never seen white kids roll a hoop and try and throw sticks through it, or throwing a spear. I guess everyone learns to play with what they have.

Some of the kids had brought me gifts and I was embarrassed about opening them. I wasn't used to getting wrapped gifts from friends, just maybe at Christmas time. Sandy got me a necklace with a gold arrowhead on it. This I really liked and put it on, and got teased by Larry and Billy about being engaged. I just smiled and took it. I didn't really mind as long as Sandy wasn't too concerned. The party lasted a long time and finally Mom said she had to go back over to Grandfathers, and I should come with her and feed the animals.

I thanked everyone, especially Sandy and her folks. Then we drove out to Grandfathers and Mom went inside, while I went out and fed Horse and Dog. I gave them water and cleaned the barn as best as I could. I could use the arm now, even though it was still in a cast. I just couldn't bend it. I walked out to the chicken coup to feed the chickens and gather the eggs, as I came in the door the old rooster saw me and flew up onto the roost.

His neck was bent sideways, and he stood there and cackled at me.

I got real brave and was dancing around taunting him, telling him what a great brave that Two Bears was, and how I didn't have any fear of him, or anything else. About that time an old hen flew off the nest in back of me cackling; I jumped sideways with fear, and fell over the feed trough, landing on my broken arm, right in the middle of a bunch of fresh chicken manure. My arm hurt like blazes and I had chicken manure all over me. The old rooster got excited and flew up higher on the roost and made a cackling sound that sounded a lot like laughter. (Can a chicken laugh?) That dang rooster had won again.

I got up and tried to clean myself up, but just smeared that stinking stuff worse than it was. I hated to go in the house like this. I got what few eggs there were and took them into grandmother's kitchen. She took one look at me and asked what happened, so I told them I tripped and fell over the feed trough, and hurt my broken arm again. I neglected to tell them I had been teasing the old rooster, and that a hen had scared me. How would it look for the great 'Two Bears' to be scared by an old hen?

Mom got a pan of water, and a washcloth, and washed me up as best she could. My cast was filthy, and my arm hurt. She took me by the hospital on the way home. The doctor took the cast off and x-rayed my arm. He said that I hadn't re-broken it, and that he was going to leave the cast off, and give me a removable one, so that I could take a shower, but for me to be sure and wear the cast all the time, except when I was bathing. Mom asked me on the way home if that old rooster had been after me again?

I said "Sort of!" She laughed and said, "He is going to be the death of you yet Johnny!"

I said. "Or I will be the death of him." We both laughed and I said, "I should have finished him off when I had him down the last time."

When I got home I took a good hot shower and washed my arm, the skin was all funny looking, just like my foot that had been under the cast. I thought about that old hen scaring me and I had to laugh. I had been so intent on teasing that old rooster I had forgotten about the other chickens. I guess I deserved what I got.

All the football games were over for the year and with my injured arm I couldn't play basketball if I wanted to. I wasn't a very good basketball player anyway. I could move fast but just didn't have the experience in shooting and handling the ball. I spent most of my time studying, since my grades had slipped a little with the school I had missed; and playing football had taken some of my study time too. I wanted to be the best student in my class, so I worked on new ways to study so that I could remember things. I made me some small cards then I would write questions on one side, and the answers on the other, of any hard problems or questions I had, then I could review them no matter where I was. I did this and carried them with me so that I could study them any time I wanted to. This helped me a lot.

I also went to the library quite often, but that was mostly because Sandy went there too. Christmas was coming up in a few weeks and I wanted to get Sandy something special. I really didn't know what I wanted to get her, but it had to be something like the necklace she gave me. I looked around a lot and found an Indian head that had been carved out of an Indian head nickel, and was on a silver chain. Only thing was I didn't have enough money to buy it. I asked Bob if he had anything I could do to make some money. Wrong thing to do! Now I had to explain to him why I wanted it. I was too embarrassed at first but finally got up enough nerve to tell him why I needed the money. He laughed at me and said, "Next, John you will be wanting to buy a ring."

Bob gave me the money and told me he would find something for me to do to earn it. I showed the necklace to Mom and she asked me, just how serious I was about this little girl? I told her we were just good friends, that she had given me the arrowhead necklace, and I wanted to give her something nice in return.

Bob and his friend had a late season elk and bear tag and asked me if I wanted to go hunting with them again: of course I jumped at the chance. I loved sleeping in the tent and eating out over a campfire. We spent the next couple of weeks getting ready to go. It would be during the Christmas break so I wouldn't miss any school. I tried to keep all of my grades up so that I could go, and Mom was taking me out to Grandfathers every weekend I was now able to take care of the animals.

I hadn't ridden Horse for a long time so I took him out for a run. We went clear to the river and back up over some high country to get back to Grandfathers. I had only been this way once before, and that was with Grandfather.

I saw some really big mule deer bucks up along the high rim rocks, but we didn't have tags for that area. It was almost dark by the time I got back and I had to brush Horse and grain him and feed the chickens. Guess who was waiting for me when I went into the coop. That old rooster! He took one look at me and flew back up onto the roost, his neck was still crooked and he acted funny. I didn't tease him this time, and I checked all the nests to make sure no old hens were behind me. I gathered all the eggs, went in and washed up as I was going to spend the night. Grandmother had dinner almost ready and a fresh pie was sitting there cooling. I went in and sat with Grandfather, he had just gotten the cast off his leg and was still walking with one crutch.

He said "John I am glad you finally decided to come stay all night. I haven't had any pie since you have been gone." The old cat jumped up on me I pet him and listened to him purr. Then Grandmother called us to come eat and I had to go wash my hands again. After we ate, Grandmother gave us a slice of apricot pie, with ice cream on it. She said that it was always my father's favorite pie. I remembered him telling me about craving apricots while he was in Korea. So I told them the story, and they sat and listened, but I am sure they had heard it before.

I hadn't brought any books with me so I could only read the notes I had on the cards that were in my pocket. I studied them while we watched some movie that Grandmother liked. I couldn't seem to get interested in it, so I finally went to bed.

Bob came out to pick me up and he had bought me a new rifle with a scope on it. He said that he had ordered it for my birthday; only it didn't get here in time. We took it out back by the rocks and set up a target. Bob told me not to get to close to the scope as the recoil would kick it back and cut my eye. I was scared the first time I shot it but I did manage to hit the target. Bob made me load and unload it several times and to always put the safety on each time I put a shell in the chamber. I liked shooting it and was able to hit the target every time. We took the gun back in the house and he showed me how to take it apart and clean it.

Grandfather got up, and hobbled into the bedroom; he came out with a large hunting knife, which he handed to me. He said, "If you're going to be a hunter you need a good knife." It was in a leather sheaf that hooked onto your belt. He instructed me on how to cut with it, and to always cut away from your body in case it slipped so you wouldn't cut yourself. He also told me that the knife had belonged to my father, and to take good care of it.

Bob said that he had bought me an elk tag and a hunting license, so now I could hunt with them on this trip. I sure hoped that Mom knew about this. I didn't want to get all excited and have her put the damper on it. I thanked Bob, and talked all the way home. I was so excited that I couldn't wait to get to school and tell Billy about it.

CHAPTER XVIII

I met Billy at school and told him all about the new rifle I had gotten for my birthday. He was going to go hunting with his dad and his uncle too. We spent the day talking about camping and going hunting. It was the Christmas season at school when everyone gets sort of silly, and not much gets done. I don't know why they even have school in December. They should gives us the whole month off, and make us start two weeks early, and go two weeks later in the summer. When I get in charge I will change it.

Bob and I had all our gear packed and were ready to go. We were going to leave as soon as I got out of school on Friday. Jim, Bob's friend was going with us. I was real excited about being able to hunt. I had never been elk hunting before but the thought of shooting a bear didn't thrill me any, so I told Bob I didn't want to hunt a bear. He just laughed at me and said I probably wouldn't see one anyway.

Friday was a mad house at school; everyone was running around wishing people a Merry Christmas, and giving people little gifts. I gave Sandy the necklace but told her not to open it until Christmas. She said that she couldn't wait, and quickly tore it open. She seemed real happy and hugged me and gave me a little peck on the cheek. I looked around to see who was watching. Everyone was too busy doing his or her own thing to notice, so I got by with that one. I fastened the chain around her neck, for her. Her hair felt so soft to the touch and her perfume sure smelled great. I told her that I was going hunting with Bob and would be gone a few days.

We talked for a while and then she took off to show her necklace to her friends. I gathered up all my books and headed for home, as I knew

Bob and Jim would be waiting. We had packed all our gear so was ready to leave as soon as I changed clothes. Mom made me a sandwich to eat on the way, and we were off. We drove for about two hours and it was dark when we got to the place we were going to camp. Bob lit a lantern and I scrounged up wood, while he and Jim set up the big tent.

It wasn't long until we had a campfire going and a fire in the tent stove. We ate hot dogs, and hot pork and beans for dinner, and had a piece of pie that mom had sent with us. I crawled into my sleeping bag and snuggled down nice and warm; the cot I was sleeping on felt kind of rickety, but I was asleep before I knew it. The next thing I knew Bob was shaking me awake; we ate cold cereal for breakfast and waited for it to get light out. Bob made me hunt with him the first day. We saw several cow elk but nothing with antlers.

We returned to camp about two. Jim had killed a spike bull about a mile from camp. He had quartered it up and had all but two pieces hanging in camp. I stayed and watched camp while they went after the rest of it. I fed the camp robbers some breadcrumbs and gathered up a big stack of wood. There were broken limbs laying everywhere so it wasn't hard to find wood. My arm was healing up good now, so I no longer needed the cast.

Bob and Jim soon came in carrying the rest of Jim's elk. He was really happy that he would have some meat for winter. We hung Jim's elk meat up high enough so that a bear couldn't get to it, then ate a sandwich and went for a drive. We drove to an area about three miles from camp where a stream cut through two steep hills. Bob had seen a lot of elk in this area before and wanted to hunt it. The plan was for Jim to drop us off up high and I would follow the stream down through the cut, to where a road crosses it, and Jim would pick me up there. Bob would hunt the high ridge down toward the stream, and meet us on the road somewhere further down.

We went back to camp, ate a bowl of soup and a sandwich and

turned in, as everyone was pretty tired. Bob and Jim were scaring off the wild animals as soon as they went to bed. I lie there listening to them snore, they could never seem to get together; finally I heard the alarm clock go off, and got up as soon as Bob lit the lantern. We ate cold cereal for breakfast then Bob made me two sandwiches and gave me an apple to carry in my pack. He made sure I had matches and a small flashlight, and a bunch of other stuff including a couple of big plastic bags that I could use in case it rained, and it looked like it was going to. I took eight shells for my rifle and put my knife on my belt. I already had a small bottle of water in my pack from the day before. Bob gave me a long piece of rope and told me to use it to tie the elk's leg back while I field dressed it. I had never even dressed out a deer, but had watched him do it a couple of times. He stressed that it was very important to get the entrails out of an elk, and prop the body cavity open, so that it would cool out fast.

I thought 'Sure, I am really going to do all of this', I wanted and hoped that I could get one, but wasn't too sure about the dressing out part.

After breakfast we all piled into Jim's pickup and he drove us to the top of the mountain. Bob walked with me until we came to a stream, then he told me to follow the stream down hill until I came to a bridge, and that would be where Jim would pick me up. Bob said it should take me four or five hours to get there if I walked slow and hunted hard. He told me not to lose sight of the stream that way I couldn't get lost. Bob crossed the stream and headed up the ridge to the left of me. I stood there for a while listening to the quietness of the forest, the bubbling sounds made by the little stream, and a few birds calling to each other. I liked it out in the forest.

I loaded my rifle, but didn't put a round in the chamber. Bob didn't want me walking with a loaded gun. I had been walking for about ten minutes when I heard a shot. I must have jumped a foot in the air as it was from pretty close by. I knelt down and waited for about ten minutes more, in case some elk came running by. I had started walking again when I saw some elk crossing the stream about a hundred yards ahead of me. I was really excited now. I put a shell in the chamber, put the safety on and crept toward where I had seen the elk crossing.

When I found their tracks I looked them over good, and could see spots of blood across the stream where they had crossed. I walked over and knelt down and ran my hand over the fresh red blood on the rocks. I stayed there for a long time waiting for someone to come along trailing the elk. They were headed up the ridge toward Bob, so I decided to follow the blood trail. It turned and went along the side of the hill going up the creek on the opposite side of where I had come down. I followed it up and over the ridge; I had seen several elk just ahead of me, and just knew I would find a wounded bull any minute. I followed them down into a deep valley that was covered with heavy timber then back up along another ridge.

It started raining so I stopped and put one of the plastic bags over me cutting a hole for my head and arms. It started raining real hard and I took shelter under some big cedar trees that grew in a clump along the hillside. I waited there for almost an hour then decided to follow the tracks some more, but it had rained so much that I couldn't find the blood trail now, and most of the tracks looked old. I decided I had better get back to the creek and follow it down. I turned to go but the trees were so tall that everything looked the same. I could feel the fear coming up in my throat as near panic gripped me. I realized I was lost.

I took off running up and over the ridge that I thought I had just crossed. I ran, and ran until I was exhausted. Finally I made myself calm down. I didn't know if I was going the right way or not. I couldn't even see the valley for all the trees and brush. Everything looked the same. I climbed back to the top of the ridge but still couldn't see anything; the rain was coming down harder now, so I stopped under a big fir tree and sat there trying to think of what I should do.

Bob had always told me if I ever got lost to just stay where I was and to make myself comfortable, and wait for someone to find me. Only they would be looking downstream and I had gone back upstream and over several ridges from where I was supposed to be. I had no idea where I was. I had never been in this area before, and didn't even look at a map to see where we would be hunting. I listened and all I could hear was the patter of the rain as it continued to fall harder. I looked around and found a huge cedar log with lots of loose bark on it. I peeled the bark off in long slabs and propped them up against the log. By over-lapping them I had a rain tight shelter. I blocked one end shut to keep the wind from blowing through; I pulled some fir branches down and piled them inside to sit on so as to keep me off the wet ground. I looked for dry fir needles and cones so that I could start a fire; and piled a lot of dead wood in front of the shelter. I had kept myself busy so as not to be so scared. I knew I was in trouble with Bob for leaving the stream. I should have marked my trail. I sat inside my crude shelter and ate one of the sandwiches. This was a good place to stay but it was in so dense of a forest that no one could ever see me. I made up my mind to stay here until the rain quit, then I would mark a trail down the side of the mountain; in case I was going the wrong way I could find my way back to here. I would do this until I found the little stream; It was only about a three hours walk from it. So I would search a half day each day, in a different direction until I found it. I worked and pulled as many branches under the bark as I could. I got a small fire going and dried out a little bit. The smoke kept blowing inside my crude shelter and choking me. The big fir tree kept a lot of the rain off; I wished I had built the shelter closer to the tree, and I would do that as soon as the rain quit. Bob had made me put a sweatshirt inside my pack and I was glad of that. I put it on and pulled the garbage bag back over me. I sat there and piled sticks on the fire, trying to dry my feet, as they had gotten wet crossing one of the little streams.

The wind was blowing and the rain kept pouring down. I knew it was going to be a cold lonely night, and that Bob and Jim would be out all night trying to find me. I tried to stay awake and listen for a gunshot, or someone hollering, but the wind was making so much noise that I couldn't hear anything.

I finally fell asleep listening to the rain and wind. I would wake up ever so often and pile more sticks on the fire. The rain was now running off the log and dripping on me so I crawled inside the other garbage bag and listened to the drops hit the plastic. I was thinking that if Bob heard the shots that I heard, he might find the trail where I followed the elk, thinking that it was me that had fired the shot. I lay there and slept in short naps and dreamed weird dreams. I would be afraid when I would wake up. I talked to myself; I must not let fear get a grip on me. I had run all morning, just because of panic, I didn't even know where I was running to, but I wanted to get there fast. I know that fear can confuse you, and confusion can kill you if you let it. I am "Two Bears" an Indian warrior. No Indian I know of has ever gotten lost, or at least admits to being lost. I have a gun and a knife I can survive out here until I find my way.

When I awoke it was light out and my fire had almost completely died out. I piled little sticks on it until the smoke was choking me. It was still a light misty rain and a blanket of heavy fog draped the trees. I knew I would have to move slowly and mark my trail every few feet, or I would really get lost in this fog. I ate the apple for breakfast and saved the sandwich. I would eat half of it tonight. I had drunk most all of my water so I would look for a clean source today, which shouldn't be any trouble, up this high on the mountain.

I remembered that the wind was blowing in my face as I started out down the stream. So I would go into the wind today. I took my knife and rifle, and headed out leaving my pack hung in the tree so that it could be seen from down the hill if the fog ever rose. I broke off a branch and let it hang down every few steps. This took a lot of time but I could follow them back to my camp. I crossed over a little stream and up over a ridge that I thought I had crossed the day before. In the fog everything looked strange and you couldn't see very far. I guessed I had been walking for about four hours as I climbed to the top of another ridge and waited for a while listening for sounds. All I could hear was the drops of water falling from the trees. I raised my rifle and fired a shot into the air, and listened as it echoed across the canyons and hills. I waited for a long time and never heard a sound. I wished I had brought more ammunition, as I should fire a shot after dark; they say sound carries farther after dark. I didn't have a watch but guessed it to be in the afternoon. I slowly made my way back toward camp. The broken branches were easy to follow. It didn't seem like it took me very long to get back but it was getting dark. I was really hungry. I worked at finding and carrying wood for my fire. I drank from a small stream on the way back and filled my water bottle.

I ate half of my sandwich, cheating a little by eating the biggest half. I drank a lot of water and lay down, I must have slept a long time for it was dark when I woke up, and my fire was just a few glowing embers. I got up and piled more wood on it, the rain had stopped and the wind was blowing from a different direction, so I marked that in my mind and would search that way when daylight came. I could see the stars and found the big dipper. By looking straight up along the bowl, aligning up the two stars that form she side of the bowl away from the handle I could find the North Star directly above them. Now I knew which direction North was but I still had no way of knowing which way to go. If Grandfather had been here he could tell what time it was by looking at the stars. I had traveled west the day before so I would go south today. I drew me a direction map in the dirt under the tree by firelight. Tomorrow I would pick landmarks and try to go in a straight direction as much as possible.

As soon as my fire blazed up again I put a big stick on it and lay back down, I couldn't sleep at first but I awoke and it was daylight. The clouds were gone and the sun was shining through the trees. I picked a big tree south of me and walked toward it breaking limbs as I went. I made my way like this down into a valley with a clear meadow and trees all around it. I found a stream that was running lots of water, but I was on the wrong side of it, for it to be the stream I wanted. I walked down it for a few miles hoping it would run into a bigger stream. I watched the sun and as it started down I headed back. I was really hungry now, as I hadn't eaten the half sandwich for breakfast, so I did have that waiting for me. I drank as much water as I could. I found some elderberry bushes with a few berries that the birds hadn't gotten yet. They were bitter and sour, but I ate all of them I could find.

It was getting late in the day and I was starved when I got back to camp. I ate the sandwich as slow as I could knowing that this was the last food that I had. I waited until dark and everything was still, then I fired another shot from my rifle. I waited and I thought I heard a shot or was it an echo? 'No it was a distant shot!' I waited and listened but didn't hear anything else. I was really tired and getting weak from not eating. I went to sleep early, and didn't wake up until the birds were scolding each other around my camp.

I got up and drank some water and figured I would go east this morning. I needed to look for food along the way, I knew some plants that were eatable, but didn't know if they grew this far up the mountain. I lined up a hilltop east of me and headed for it I was going up the side of a ridge when I saw and heard a helicopter coming toward me. I just stood there like a dummy, when it went by. Then I realized that they were probably looking for me by now. I cursed myself for being so dumb. I took my tee shirt off so I would have something white to wave at them if they came back by. I saw them again several times but they were always a long ways from me.

As I started down into a creek bottom I saw a small deer watching me. I watched it for a moment then realized that this was food. I put a shell into the rifle and took careful aim and fired, the deer fell, and I ran over and made sure it was dead. I field dressed it and saved the liver; I put the deer over my back and carried it back to camp. I put the liver on a stick and cooked it over the fire. I don't like liver but this tasted pretty good even if it was half raw. I stayed there in my camp cutting it up, and cooking strips of deer meat.

I listened for the helicopter but it never came back over. I ate so much meat that I was almost sick so I lay down and it was dark again when I woke up. I drank all the water in my bottle and sat by the fire and thought about the trouble I was in. I don't know how many days I have been out here but think it is four. I will go east again tomorrow as I only went out for about two hours, it would be fast going in the morning as the trail is well marked down to where I shot the deer.

I moved out again at first light taking my pack with some dried deer meat in it; at least I would travel on a full stomach. I made good time getting to where I killed the deer, and then I headed straight up and over a ridge top. I could see what I thought was a road or part of a road about ten miles from me on a ridge side. I marked a straight line and headed for it. I crossed a little stream and went up and over another ridge. I couldn't see the road from here. I checked the sun and headed what I thought was east, it was getting late in the day when I hit a stream, that I think is the one I was supposed to follow down to the road. I walked downstream until I found the place that Bob and I had split up, at last I know where I am; I think!

Only thing is it is getting too dark to travel and it looks like it is going to rain again. I look for a big log, or tree to make a shelter. I am careful not to lose sight of the stream. I find a big cedar tree and pull the limbs down around me tying them in place with the rope. The rain is pouring down now, and I get the plastic bag and put it over me again and crawl into the other one. I eat a few strips of dried deer meat and huddle shivering close to the tree. I sleep in naps, waking up and listening to the pouring rain. I am staying pretty dry but some drops get down my neck from soaking through my hat. I can hear the little stream roaring as more and more water drains off the hills into it. My rifle is soaked but it hasn't started to rust yet. I will fire it come morning to keep rust from forming in the barrel.

I am up at first light and fire a shot from the rifle. I don't hear anything so I start down the little creek, which is running bank full now with rainwater. It is pouring rain and the wind is blowing hard as I make my way down the stream bank. I walk for what seems like hours. I am getting soaked from the knees down, the old plastic bag, is keeping me pretty dry on the upper part, but it has a few holes that is letting in some wet spots.

I stop under a big yew wood thicket, to rest and eat some more deer meat. It is cold and wet and soaked with rainwater, but I still eat it. I am sitting there eating and I hear a shot that sounds like it is right behind me. I run out of the thicket and look all around. I can't see anyone, so I start on down the creek. I stop and decide to shoot my rifle. I put a shell in the chamber and fire a shot into the air, almost instantly I hear another shot, only I can't tell where it is coming from.

The wind is swirling the rain around in circles. I hear still another shot, but can't decide from what direction it is coming from, so I continue walking on down the stream. I don't know for sure if this is where I am supposed to be, but I will walk until dark, or until I find the road.

I hear more shooting but don't seem to have mind enough to answer back again; for some reason I don't think they are for me. I have now lost all fear of being lost. I am on a mission to get to a road and that is all that I am thinking of. My body is numb from the rain and cold, my feet feel like they aren't attached to my body and I am just walking on stubs. I am not in any pain or suffering. I am just a body moving through, and around wet fir trees, current bushes, and yew wood thickets. I jump each time I hear a rifle shot, only I don't even look around to see where they are coming from. The plastic bag has long since been torn from my body, I am cold and wet but don't feel it. My body shivers with each icy blast from the wind, and every small fir tree I touch sends showers of cold water down my body. I can hear my feet sloshing in my boots. I am unaware of the rifle I still hold, grasping the wet slippery wood stock firmly in my hand. I have long lost my hat and my jet-black hair lies plastered to the sides of my scalp with rivulets of water pouring down my neck. My body is so cold and wet there is no feeling left in it. I look down at my hand on the arm I had broken, it is all shriveled up and blue, but I am still clutching the rifle. I shift it over to my good hand, and it feels cold and heavy. As the day goes on I walk without much feeling but I am still following the stream.

I climb up a steep bank to get around a cement and wood structure, realizing that I am standing in the middle of a bridge watching the water cascade under it. My mind is numb as to where I am; only instinct leads me down this road. In my mind I will walk on all night to where I do not know. I can barely keep going. I am starting to feel the cold, as I notice the steam coming up from my body.

Someone is talking to me; they ask if anyone has found him yet. I just stand there and stare. I hear a woman's voice saying he is freezing get him in the truck, and let him get warm. I sit in the truck and start shaking so violently that I can't control it. I feel a warm towel being rubbed through my hair. Someone said, "I think this is the boy they are looking for!" I can't answer. I am not asleep, neither am I awake, my body is exhausted the cold grips me as my temperature drops.

I manage to say, "Tell Bob I am back." The next thing I hear is the popping sound of a helicopter. I try to get up to wave my shirt. "I am here!" Will they see me? Once again blackness envelops me. I am moving but it's not my own power that is carrying me. I reach for my rifle and someone takes my hand. I can't lose the rifle. I am 'Two Bears' the one they call 'Chief'. I must get back. No Indian ever gets lost!

CHAPTER XIX

I woke up with bright lights shining at me, and warm blankets surrounding me. I was shaking so hard my teeth were clicking together, and someone was talking to me, but I couldn't make them out. I was so cold that I couldn't move, and the heat from the blankets was making me sick. I tried to move the blankets but my arms were tied down; I tried to kick and there were straps on my feet. I lie there trying to feel for the rifle I must not loose it. I wanted to move back from the fire; I was wet and freezing but the fire was too hot. I tried to open my eyes but the sun was too bright; someone kept talking to me. There was something stuck in my throat I tried to cough it up and it kept gagging me.

Someone was rubbing my arms and legs. I felt as if I was falling into a deep pit, I could see the blackness of it, as I teetered on the edge. I was so cold and the fire was too warm, I wanted to scoot back from it. I could hear voices calling Johnny, Johnny! But I couldn't answer. My teeth were chattering so hard I was getting sick, and the thing in my throat was choking me. I could no longer hear the wind or feel the rain. I felt I was moving, but I was lying still. I wanted to get up but was tied down, where was I?

I could see Grandfather standing beside the Great Warrior, they were both looking down at me; suddenly I was with them I could see myself lying on a white bed with people working on me. The Great Warrior turned to me and said, "It is not your time Two Bears, you must go back, as you have much yet to do, you must fight this battle and many more." Suddenly my body jumped against the straps that held me. I opened my eyes and looked into the bright lights that were shining down on me.

Many hands were holding onto me. I could see my grandfather and my mother, as well as many people I didn't know all dressed in blue gowns and funny hats. I wanted to laugh, but my teeth were still chattering and the thing in my throat was choking me. I tried to cough it out again then someone pulled it free. I reached out and took Grandfathers hand. I asked, "Can you find my rifle?" He grinned and said, "It is safe Johnny; we put it away."

Mom reached over and ran her hand through my hair, "How are you doing?" she asked.

"I am too hot!" I said. My teeth were still chattering, and my throat was so sore I could hardly talk or swallow.

I heard someone say, "He is a tough boy to survive out there in all this rain for six days; how he kept from dieing of exposure, and hypothermia I don't understand. Most people would perish within a few days in weather like that. And to have the ability to find his way back out of a place he had never been, he is truly a remarkable boy." I went to sleep thinking of how nice it is to hear good things about ones self.

When I awoke I was in a room by myself with just my mom sitting by my bed, and it was so hot in there I was about to melt. At least I could kick the covers off, as I was no longer tied down. Mom looked at me and asked how I was doing? Next she wanted to know how I got lost. I told her I wasn't lost I just didn't know where the road was. I said, "Mom an Indian never gets lost." she smiled at me and said, "Well, I know one little Indian boy that sure was missing for almost a week."

About that time Bob came into my room wearing a hospital gown like they had tied on to me. Mom said, "Johnny I want you to know that Bob almost died out there looking for you. He stayed out in all that rain for three days looking for you; until he got so sick that Jim brought him in here. Then Jim and some of his friends walked all over that mountain looking for you. Where were you?"

I told them about following the wounded elk and seeing them several times, until I got turned around and went over the mountain the wrong way. "Once I realized I didn't know which way to go, I made a shelter from cedar bark, and built a fire. I killed a deer and dried the meat so I wasn't too hungry. Then I marked a trail from camp each day until I found the stream. I was scared at first and ran for a long ways, until I realized I didn't know where I was running too."

Bob told me that when I didn't show up at the road and they had heard the same shot I did, and figured it was me shooting; that Jim and he, walked all the way up the creek to where we parted. Then they searched all the way back to the road. They spent the rest of the night there at the bridge in the truck. The next day it was so wet and foggy that he walked back up the stream firing his rifle every thirty minutes. Jim drove along the road thinking that you might have come out along it someplace else. When you hadn't showed up by noon on the second day, Jim drove into town and got the sheriff and the search and rescue. On the third day they sent up a helicopter, to look for you.

"Johnny there was over a hundred people searching for you for three days; most of them had given up and went home, when you finally came out and were found walking down the road. The couple that found you weren't even part of the search party, they had just driven up to see if they could help."

Bob said, "John you done a lot of things wrong, but you did some right, and that is why you survived. I don't know how you stayed dry, and kept from freezing to death up there. Your body temperature was so low when they brought you in, that none of the doctors thought you had much of a chance to survive."

I told him I was sorry that I had caused so much trouble, and worry for everyone. "I just didn't think, until it was too late. I had been so excited when I saw the elk, and then found blood. I just knew that they would go over the ridge in front of you. I was lost before I realized it. I knew everyone would be looking in the wrong place for me, for I had gone back up stream and over the ridge behind you. After I settled down and got over the fear, I figured I could find my way but that it would take a few days. I had only trailed the elk for a couple of hours, so after I got a shelter made I knew I could search out from there and eventually find the stream again. I was very careful to mark my trail after that so that I could get back each time." I told them about seeing the helicopter, and taking my tee shirt off to wave at them but that they never came back.

Bob gave me a hug and said for me to get well, and we would do it again. Mom started to protest but changed her mind. I felt fine and was ready to go home, but the doctor said I had to stay until morning. I was bored lying there in that bed. I knew everyone was angry with me. I was mad at myself. I knew better than to go traipsing off through strange country and not mark my trail. I was lying there feeling sorry for myself, when Sandy and her mom came in.

Sandy came over and gave me a big hug and asked how I was feeling, embarrassed!" I said. "I am ready to go home, and I told everyone that but it didn't help.

The doctor still said, I would have to wait until tomorrow; and Bob is feeling much better so they are going to let us both go home at the same time".

Sandy's mom left her there to talk to me while she went shopping. Sandy said, that she prayed for my safety all the time I was lost. I told her I did a lot of praying too.

"After the rain stopped and the sun came out that third day, I felt like I could find my way out. Especially after I killed the deer and had food once again."

We talked about school and Christmas. I said, "This will be one Christmas I won't forget. I hate the thought of going back to school after the New Year. It will be all over school how the Indian got himself lost." We both laughed and Sandy said, "You will just have to tell them how the Indian found his way home again".

178

I was released from the hospital the next day along with Bob; but they made me stay in bed for two more days so that I didn't develop any pneumonia from my ordeal. Bob had really had a bad case of it but the doctors were able to catch it in time.

The next day we went to Grandfathers for Christmas dinner, he had just gotten the cast off his leg and said he felt twenty pounds lighter. I went out and cleaned Horses' stall. Mr. Fox had been over and done most of it. I brushed Horse down real good and gave him some grain. Dog acted strange, like he was mad at me for not being there for a while.

The old rooster still remembered me. He sat up on the roost and cackled at me his neck was still bent crooked. I guess he didn't want me to try and straighten it out for him, so he stayed up out of my reach. Grandmother had made me a big raisin pie, and told me I could take it home with me. I told Bob that being as how he hunted for me so hard, I would let him have a piece of it. He laughed and cut it in four pieces and ate a quarter of it there. Everyone laughed and when we headed home I only had one piece of pie left.

When we got home there was a huge box on our porch. It was addressed to me, from Sandy, Jill, Larry, Joe and a bunch of other kids. I picked it up and it wasn't very heavy, I took it inside and opened it, inside was another box, and another box, until I opened about ten boxes. Inside of the last one, was a compass, a map, a whistle, a mirror and a book of matches, with a list of instructions that said " If you get lost, study map real close, try and figure out where you are lost at; look in mirror to make sure it is you that is lost; blow on whistle to scare away any bears, then take compass and find south, go that way, as it is always warmer in the south, and remember don't play with matches." It was signed your friends.

This made me feel a lot better; at least my friends could see some humor in what happened. That night Bob brought in the paper and there on the front page was a picture of me standing soaking wet with my hair plastered to my face, with a headline saying. LOST BOY RELEASED FROM HOSPITAL, Expected to make full recovery, (What ever that is.)

Bob teased me and said, "They didn't say a word about me!"

Mom sat me down and discussed all the things that had happened to me and said, she should have left me out with Grandfather, but I got into trouble out there too.

Bob just laughed and said, "That is all part of growing up. He will never get lost again; this will teach him a valuable lesson."

I was glad when school started again, even if I did have to get up in front of the class and tell about my being lost. I tried to tell everyone how I did things wrong. I didn't tell them how scared I had been, or about my running around the mountain like a wild Indian. I tried to stress the important part of always going the way you are supposed to go, and to mark your trail so that you can get back. I also told them how good, wet cold half cooked deer meat is without any salt. The teacher told me she was thankful that I was back safe, and everyone joined in, and congratulated me on my survival. I joked and said, 'I had to survive to get back and look at all of you again,' then I thanked them for the survival kit they had given me for Christmas, especially the written instructions. Everyone laughed and we got back to studying.

At lunch Billy and I talked about hunting and he told me how scared he was of becoming lost. I told him to always break a little green branch as you walk along, and let it hang down, it doesn't make that much noise and you can always follow your trail back that way.

I didn't try and play basketball, as my arm was still sore, and that trek through the brush didn't help it any, since I had left the portable cast off of it. I went to some of the games that were played at our school. It looked like fun and our team was pretty good. I always sat with Sandy, which was more fun than playing ball.

We were watching one game and Sandy had been real quiet all day so I knew something was wrong.

Sandy finally told me that her father didn't want her hanging around with me, that he didn't want her to get too serious over a damn Indian. This really hurt me, I didn't know what to say, and so I just sat there, and didn't say anything. I really liked her. Being with her at school was what made going to school fun for me. I knew her father didn't want her to go riding out on the reservation with me anymore. I asked her if she ever told him that I was one of the best students in the class. I always studied hard and made good grades. I never caused any trouble, unless someone picked on me. She sat there and held onto my hand, and said, "We can still see each other, I just don't think you should come around when my father is home. And I doubt if Mom will ever let me go riding with you anymore."

I just sat there all choked up, while the sickness built up inside of me, than it commenced to turn to anger. I asked her, "What have I ever done to you or to him to make him feel this way; or is he just some prejudice person that doesn't like Indians?" My throat was so dry I wanted to heave; here I thought I had one true friend, more than that I loved her. I slowly picked up my books and walked away while she called after me. I wanted to turn around and go back, but my pride wouldn't let me.

When Friday came I asked Mom to let me go out to Grandfathers for the weekend.

I was glad to get back out there. I worked hard cleaning the barn and grooming Horse; I played with Dog some and took care of the chickens. I was hoping the old rooster would jump me as I was spoiling for a fight. I couldn't get what Sandy had said out of my mind. I may be a damn Indian to some people, but I will be the toughest and smartest damn Indian any of them have ever seen, when I am through.

I got up early on Saturday and took Horse out for a run; the more he ran the madder I got. Here I am only fourteen years old and in the eighth grade, what did her father think I was going to do; elope with her? I made up my mind that I would confront him the next time I saw him, and ask him face to face if he thought that a damn Indian wasn't good enough for his daughter. Horse was running hard and so was my mind. When we got to the river I rode Horse straight out into it, even though it was still winter. I had to cool off; and the cold water brought me back to my senses. I thought then, 'this was real smart, now I was cold and wet and had a long ride back, maybe I was just a dumb Indian.'

I rode up onto a rocky bluff and tied Horse to some brush. I was cold and shaking, but I sat out there on a rock, and thought for a while. I took off the necklace Sandy had given to me. I ran the gold chain through my fingers, and felt of the shiny gold arrowhead. I couldn't blame Sandy for what her father thought of me. I decided I would still be friends with her at school, and maybe meet her at the park. I would just stay away from her family for a while.

Why can't people see that we can't pick what race we will be, or who we will be; all we can do is work, study and be the best person we can be? I was getting cold now from the wet clothes. I got on Horse and rode hard back to Grandfathers. I grained Horse and gave him a quick rub down. I went into the house and Grandmother noticed my wet clothes, as I went into change. I just laughed and told her I went for an early swim, she never said anything else, so I didn't mention it again.

I went into where Grandfather was watching television, the old gray cat came and jumped up in my lap; he didn't care if I was an Indian or not. Maybe he was an Indian cat. I couldn't tell and I doubt if anyone else could. It is too bad people have to see colors. I don't think animals do, if they do they don't care. I sat and watched Grandfather more than I did the television. His face and skin looked like leather, from the wind and rain. He had lots of wrinkles and deep lines in his face; he really looked old since we had the wreck. Maybe all of the stuff that I had caused him to worry about was making him old.

I told him about seeing the Great Warrior again while I was in the hospital. How he and I had stood beside him, and he told me I couldn't be there yet and that I must go back.

Grandfather said, "Johnny you were a very sick boy, and sometimes when we are sick we see things that aren't as we think they are."

He said, "I am very proud of you and the way you survived out there. Most people would have run themselves crazy. You showed great knowledge, and courage the way you kept the rifle, and your knife. A lot of lost hunters have thrown away their weapons or lost them. I knew you would survive; you have many things ahead of you to do. You will fight many battles before you are my age; most of them will be battles of words and learning, so prepare yourself. This country will need strong men like you if it is going to survive. The Indian must change and learn to live like the white man. We must educate ourselves and learn to lead the whites as well as the Indian. We have been here a lot longer than the black man, but he has managed to get his people in high offices, and have a national day of honor for one of their people. This whole country once belonged to the Indian, yet there is no holiday or day of honor for the red man.

Young people like you must rise up and demand to be a part of this great nation. This country needs leaders, so Two Bears don't just set your sights on being Chief of our people; we are all Americans, and so be Chief of all the American people. Then everyone will call you "Chief".

If you liked this book! Look for "Chief the next Saga" coming to a bookstore near you soon.........

-Karl

www.ingramcontent.com/pod-product-compliance
Lightning Source LLC
Chambersburg PA
CBHW022050050726
47591CB00002B/474